Praise for *i*

"It's cynical but warm, existential but engaging, heartbreaking but peaceful."
- Reviewer on Amazon.com

"Yes, yes it's good, you're good... I believe in you... you're a good writer...now go shovel the driveway."
- Author's wife

"From the 1st few pages this book was riveting. Filled with a smart, dark sense of humor - the plot is quick paced (I couldn't put it down!) and brilliantly laid out."
-Another review from Amazon.com

"It's very nice, dear. No, I didn't read the whole thing. I really prefer mysteries set in Scotland."
-Author's mother

"I found myself vested in all of the action and all of the characters. I thought Pogodzinski masterfully intermingled broad themes with every day actions and every day people."
- Yet another review from Amazon.com

"You wrote a book?"
-Author's brother

"The actual story is incredibly intriguing, drawing on fears of the rising global tensions, religious fanaticism, and the smaller troubles of bullying and needful children."
- Review from Bookhitch.com

"Woof."
-Author's dog

Flashes and Specks

A Novel in 35 Episodes

Mark Pogodzinski

<<<>>>
A No Frills Edition
Buffalo, New York

Printed in the United States of America

Pogodzinski, Mark

Flashes and Specks/ Pogodzinski- 2nd Edition

ISBN 978-0-578-04711-9

1. Metaphysics – End of the World – Fiction.   2. Madness – New Author – No Frills – Fiction.
1. Title

No Frills Press
Buffalo, New York

For Henry and Patricia

Affection will not be gainsay'd, the sense of what
is real, the thought if after all it should prove
unreal,
The doubts of day-time and the doubts of night-
time,
the curious whether and how,
Whether that which appears so is so, or is it all
flashes
and specks?
Men and women crowding fast in the streets, if
they are not
flashes and specks what are they?

- Walt Whitman

Episode 1: The Conqueror

Blood trickles from his mouth.

It all comes down to this, as it should, the hero and the villain. All other things are meaningless, trifles set against the grand notion of good versus evil. You see that now, don't you? You see it for what it is, for the beauty of it and the simplicity. This is all there is, this is all that matters. The small things are inconsequential, because each decision, each choice is at its core this truth: you're either a hero or you're a villain. I can see that you understand. I also learned it at a young age. That's the great thing about the hero and the villain, sometimes they're not that different.

Knuckles are sore suddenly, must've hit his chin. There's blood trickling from his mouth again. It seems so bright even in the darkness.

It all started at the funeral breakfast. He was aware of it in the corner of the restaurant among the whispers and the clinking of coffee cups. He knew that he was fated to do something to help the world, combat evil, right wrongs, a childhood dream that never left his mind. It never died as so many of childhood's visions do. It clawed and scraped to remain alive, convinced of its own truth and justice.

Henry's cousin had killed himself. His family called it a tragedy and for the best in the end. Carter was different, but Henry liked him because he was honest when he was alive. Carter was the wild one, the artist without art. To Henry he was humorous, making fun of the adults, talking back, swearing at them. He told people what he thought, what he believed, the plain facts of life, the right and wrong of the world.

Henry was only thirteen when Carter slit his wrists and walked about his house, dripping blood on the carpet. His mother found him in his bed, his body white and pale in the evening gloom. Henry thinks of the scene from time to time, the horror of it. The image haunted him for months as a child, and even after his own son was born. It creeps in now and then, and is still horrible.

Henry knew Carter had attempted suicide once before. Carter had told him the story and was even proud of the scars, the white marks along his arms. He told Henry that when he first saw the blood he was terrified. Henry was sure that he wouldn't try again. It wasn't good to kill yourself. They talked about it, Carter confiding in his younger cousin, explaining the pain and the reasons why, the daily anguishes of his life. The cousins talked over comic books, both collecting and sorting after weekly trips to the local store. Carter often related his experiences to the characters in the colorful pages. Henry was happy to know that his cousin had decided to live.

And then he was gone. Henry tried to put the pieces together and solve the mystery of the sudden change. He was immensely and profoundly sad.

The funeral breakfast seemed to drag on, time slowing down for the family to gossip and mourn. Henry had just finished a piece of toast when it happened. He wasn't hungry, but his mother told him the food was paid for and he should eat, so he did. His mother was sitting next to him, speaking with a distant relation who also sat at their table. Carter was the subject of the conversation.

"He was too emotional," Aunt Barbara stated.

"Well, I'm not sure it was that," Henry's mom responded.

"Oh, it was. His parents should've watched him," Aunt Barbara continued.

"I think they did the best they could," answered Henry's mom frankly.

"I told his mother he was dangerous," Aunt Barbara said pointing her fork at Henry's mother.

"No mother wants to believe that about her child," Henry's mom said.

"I told her," said Aunt Barbara as she shook her head.

"In the end he only hurt himself," said Henry's mom.

"He should have thought of his poor mother," answered Aunt Barbara while eating a fork full of salad.

"I think he was concerned about his own pain," Henry's mom responded and sipped her coffee.

"Children don't know anything about real pain," said Aunt Barbara again pointing her fork, this time at Henry.

"Hmm."

Henry watched Aunt Barbara eat undercooked roast beef, boiled potatoes, and other half-prepared foods without pause. She seemed to be in constant motion, but not moving at all. The base of her, the center remained a part of the chair, connected forever. She nodded once at him, acknowledged he had been born and continued eating.

"Even this brunch seems wrong," observed Aunt Barbara and she waved her fork to the room as bits of potato fell to the floor.

"Hmm."

"Suicide is a sin. We shouldn't be celebrating Carter," Aunt Barbara explained.

"I think it's more for the family than for him," Henry's mom said.

"Still. All this seems too much for him," continued Aunt Barbara as she chewed and chewed.

"Too much to remember his life?" asked Henry's mom, looking at Aunt Barbara for the first time.

"To hear everyone talk, you'd think he was special," sneered Aunt Barbara.

"He was."

"Oh yes, I know he was special. I didn't mean to imply that he wasn't special. But what he did, makes this seem too grandiose for him," choked Aunt Barbara, as shades of embarrassment crept into her cheeks.

"You know," Henry's mom said through clenched teeth, as if she was almost ready. "I think I'll get some more coffee."

"Fine. I'll watch your boy," said Aunt Barbara and she smiled at Henry.

Henry remembered the times when he was told to watch Carter. It was his role at large family functions, picnics, weddings and funerals to occupy Carter and keep him out of trouble. Henry always brought his comic books and that seemed to calm his cousin, made it okay to be still in a swirling world.

Aunt Barbara continued to talk and to feed.

Henry knew his mother was waiting for Aunt Barbara to leave so she could return. It was her nature, evident to a child that she would rather retreat or run than stand. It was her way and eventually she would come back as if nothing happened.

Henry gazed around the room, noting the small clusters of people huddled in whispered conversations. They seemed to lean into each other, almost touching, but afraid to make contact, afraid the other person might be real. They spoke of Carter in the abstract, in the ethereal afterlife, Carter the ghost. The real person, the wild happy sad person ceased to be real, to be anything. He lived solely as conversation, stories and lessons, a dark tale to be told once a year at holiday time.

Rumors would grow out of Carter, he would produce more in death than he had in life.

    Cluster 1: He was depressed.

    Cluster 2: He was on medication.

    Cluster 3: Maybe he was gay.

    Cluster 2: They should sue.

    Cluster 3: Maybe he was in love

    Cluster 1: All teenagers are depressed.

    Cluster 3: I think it was a girl.

    Cluster 1: I heard there was a note.

    Cluster 2: It was a girl. It's always a girl.

    Cluster 1: A note?

    Cluster 3: Remember when he…

    Cluster 2: Remember when…

    Cluster 1: Remember…

    Henry continued to scan the room, watching and marking. In his mind he saw the scene simply: a culmination of fear and doubt, a gray area that was all too common. Carter would have hated being there. Aunt Barbara spoke again, wiping salad dressing from her mouth. She was talking about the popular story that Carter had killed himself because of an argument with his girlfriend on the bus ride home. Then Henry saw him.

    "She wasn't my girlfriend," Carter said. He was standing behind Aunt Barbara.

    Henry watched his cousin, not surprised by his presence.

    "It was a mistake, really. But I think it was for the best. I might even come back from the dead. The good superheroes never really die."

    "She's been talking about you," Henry told Carter. "She won't shut up."

    Aunt Barbara ignored Henry, preoccupied with a roll.

    "Yeah, I guess I'm the center of attention now. I think they'll forget me in time. At least most of them will."

    "I won't," Henry said.

"I know. But she will. She'll forget me until I'm brought up in conversation. I've never even talked to the whale. Remember I used to make fun of her. Fat bitch."

"Yeah."

"I should do something, so she will remember me."

Aunt Barbara put the buttered roll in her mouth. Then she started to cough. Henry watched her with interest. She quietly tried to cough with more force, attempting not to draw attention to herself. She looked about the room as signs of panic filled her eyes. Her hand spread on the table, growing faintly pale. She tapped her chest with her other hand, pressing with more force as seconds passed. Her eyes grew wider as she realized certain aspects of life and that it might end quickly. Henry observed her, noted each change as she moved from fear to terror to desperation. Her face turned to a deep red, her eyes widened and her nostrils flared. Carter stood motionless behind her. She started to beat her hands on the table. Cups and silverware jumped into the air.

The clusters of people grew louder to compensate for the distraction. Henry noted them too. No heroes in the groups, no one rushing to the rescue of an overweight woman. Carter did not smile, did not laugh, but watched with Henry, taking it all in, the epic final moments of a life. Aunt Barbara began to pound her chest in an attempt to heave the roll from her throat, her lungs starved for air. Henry tried to appreciate the fact that the woman might die, that he was witnessing her last seconds before the end. He looked at Carter.

"In the comics death is full of color and sound. It's always a cliffhanger, gotta buy the next issue to see what happens. But like I said, the really good heroes never die."

Aunt Barbara could not speak, only gag and convulse. She continued to beat the table and her chest. Henry watched with Carter, waiting for someone to help. Henry made the conscious decision not to attempt a rescue.

"Good idea. All great heroes have a gray past. You can use this instance as motivation for future deeds."

Henry considered his cousin's advice as he watched Aunt Barbara struggle, desperate to live another year, minute, second.

"She's choking!"

Carter and Henry turned to find silence in the room. All eyes were drawn to Aunt Barbara in her battle for survival. She staggered to her feet, jumped once and collapsed to the floor.

No one moved instantly. It was as if time stopped and everything froze confronted by the closeness of death. The world paused for a moment of grand reflection.

Then movement and there were suddenly people about her, pulling her to her feet. She coughed as her arms dangled. Her eyes were open, sad though, as if she had seen enough.

A hero emerged from amongst the mourners. A large man stepped behind Aunt Barbara and forced the roll from her. She expelled the morsel to the room and fell forward. It was a simple act, common. This man, larger than life, was congratulated heartily. Henry took it all in.

Carter disappeared into the crowd. Henry would see him again. Sometimes they would talk and sometimes not. As for Aunt Barbara, she died a month later. She fell off a ladder while hanging wallpaper, renovations to celebrate not dying. Her body went undiscovered for several days.

Episode 2: Countdowns and Crossovers

He's not crying yet. Maybe he won't.

You know that there were others before you. Some fought and some didn't. Perhaps they knew the end was coming and they accepted it. They knew that this had to happen. You see, no matter what they do to the hero, the villain always suffers more. The audience demands it. They cheer for it. They want the villain to pay. Yet, in most cases the physical pain doesn't compare to the emotional pain the villain experiences. The audience never really understands what the villain goes through.

The sounds are different with him. The pitch of the slap is higher. It stings. Not like the others. He hasn't started crying yet.

"She'll come back," Henry's father says as he sits back and pats his stomach. "I mean, look at your mom and me. It'll happen."

"Thanks, Dad."

"You still have Arthur. He should be your top priority."

Henry looks at his son, as the boy swirls mashed potatoes and gravy, taking great care that the mixture is a certain color, a specific color. Every ounce of his concentration, every bit of him is wrapped up in the mashed potatoes and gravy.

"Yeah."

"He needs you so much and now that Diana is gone…" Henry's father looks to his own plate.

"Now Bruce, don't start with that," Henry's mother says, sensing the change in atmosphere.

"I'm sorry, Henry. I didn't mean to bring it up like that." He pauses and smiles. "She'll come back. Look at your mom and me."

"It's all right, Dad. She isn't dead. We can talk about her. We were married."

"You're still married," Henry's mother interjects.

"Yeah. It's just that she's gone and brooding over her and not talking about her doesn't mean anything."

Henry's father smiles quickly, looking at his grandson. "It'll work out. You'll see. I'm sure of it. This will have a happy ending."

The table relaxes with a general sigh of contentment. The nervous energy dissipates.

Eventually the family adjourns to the living room, save for Henry's mother. She remains in the kitchen to clean the dishes. In time she rejoins the family and sits next to her husband on the couch. Henry watches them as his son flicks the television remote, thirty seconds and then something else. The living room strobes with subtle movements: a kiss, a touch, a sigh. Henry sees it all, the story unfolding.

He remembers when his parents were separated. It was just after Henry had graduated from college. He knew his father was in pain; the old man, anguish filled, betrayed finally after several less devastating incidents. Henry was always aware of the feelings of others, taking their wants and needs into account before his own. In particular he was acute to the pain of others. He likes to think of this understanding as akin to a superpower, empathy taken to the last extent.

His father's pain was too overwhelming though, the loss, the emptiness nearly consumed him. Henry could only watch, too afraid to use his power and understand the dynamics of his father's sorrow. He might have been swallowed also, taken to a deep place with no hope.

His father became more and more remote, forcing each conversation back to his wife and the fundamental question of why. Was it the snoring that made her leave? Was it the lack of physical attention? Was it him, his very being that drove her away? Henry's father remained in darkness, moping, unwilling to explore the world without a companion, without his wife, without that part of him. He would not acknowledge cheer or anything that could be considered joyous. He did not smile even when his son, the quiet child, brought home a beautiful woman named Diana, the lovely, perfect picture of a young woman, beaming ray of light, lighting the darkness of the world. But even this beacon of goodness, this example to all downtrodden men, this definition of grace could not resurrect Henry's father from his malaise.

Henry's mind turned from his father to this Diana, princess, goddess, chosen to bear divinity to the world. He fell into her and was happy. His father was abandoned again, only this time by blood, by his own son. The old man grew more morose, spiteful at the world, lashing out in vengeance as if he felt the basic disappointment of all people. Henry ignored his father and left him to his own world of self-pity and disgust. Diana was there and the light of the world called to him.

Then on a Thursday Henry's mother came back. She had been gone eighteen months and then she came back. Henry's father was elated, vindicated in his manic devotion to his wife and her memory. On Saturday there was a party, welcome back, meet Henry's girlfriend, a celebration of new things. Henry kept waiting for his father to exact some revenge on his wayward partner. He wanted his father to do something for the sake of all broken men, all stereotypical men held together by strong women. But there was no such scene, nothing at all close. His parents smiled and touched and kissed and hugged as if there had been no rift, no chasm between them. She had come back and that was all.

She would repeat her pattern, nothing as extreme as a legal procedure. But she would leave and return without explanation. She would disappear for a week or so and then return and nothing.

Henry watches his parents on the couch, his father holding his mother tightly. The Kent family spends Sunday evening together in front of the television. At eight o'clock Arthur is ready to leave. Good-byes are spoken, awkward hugs and contact. Henry ignores his power and walks out into the growing cold of winter.

Arthur is finally asleep after his routine of arranging pillows and blankets and working himself to comfort and ease. He sleeps very still with only a hint of movement in his chest and subtle disturbances of air around his mouth and nose. He will remain in this position until six-seventeen in the morning when he will go to the bathroom and then he will wait in the kitchen until his father rises and breakfast is prepared.

Henry watches his son, seemingly calm, eyes closed, peaceful. He would kiss Arthur and make him know he is loved, but such a break in protocol would be a disaster of epic proportion. He simply shuts off the light and goes to bed.

Without Diana, Henry's bed is cold. He lies in the middle, stretching his arms to the edges and wrapping his fingers around the mattress. She was here once. The left side of the bed was hers, near the table, a glass of water waiting. He remembers how she asked him not to touch her during the night, in particular if she were dreaming. It made her uncomfortable to wake abruptly from a dream. It would leave the vision unresolved she told him. He would touch her anyway and feel her warm body in the night. She never said anything. He can still smell her, embedded in the sheets, in the pillows, in the room.

She was overly attractive in the beginning. Her personality was infectious, her beauty enchanting. He was jealous of the attention she garnered from other men. He was physical with these suitors, those men whose eyes washed over her arms, legs, and face. He thinks of those times at night, touching her side of the bed. He was happy then, protecting her, showing affection through physical threats. He was young and she was young, both looking to settle down, determined that this was it, this was the one. They discussed the future very early on in the relationship, both in their early twenties, all other relationships gone wrong. Too young, too wrapped up in the pleasure, he thinks, determined to convince each other that this was love.

He might have loved them all before her. He admits that to the shadows of the bedroom. Each one before Diana. He thinks of the one from high school, the poor broken girl, the first one, lovely little thing. She was dangerous because she cried at night in his arms. He might have loved her if not for his youth and his need to leave the small town and know the world. He thinks of her, naked in his boyhood room, entangled in his arms and legs, wanting more and nothing else in the world. He can't remember her name and the room grows darker.

Episode 3: Ominous Numbers

"Math is perfect. Math is pristine. Math is without compromise. Math is brutal in its beauty and necessity to reach a concrete conclusion. Math is the secret of the universe. Math is the answer to all questions. Math is simply the basis of all life."

It's a short speech once given by Henry's college professor that Henry repeats each year to his eighth grade classes. The subject has appealed to Henry since his early childhood, grammar school and the burgeoning education of the boy. He was drawn to math, enthralled by the wonder of it, the intricate connection of numbers and symbols. He investigated math in all its forms: as the basis of music, theories of light and color, wavelength at certain frequencies, the name of God in numbers, the Celtic god who could only exist in the lap of a virgin. Yet the aspect he found most intriguing was the lack of emotion. There is nothing to clutter the senses in terms of desire or the ugliness associated with Literature or History. There is no individual bending the world to darkness or light. There is no confusion as to what will happen. There is only right and wrong with math, only the answer, nothing to cloud the eventual truth.

But since the departure of Diana, Henry has been less inclined to be enthusiastic about imparting knowledge. There was joy once. To see in the face of a child acknowledgement, the answer is known and the world becomes less frightening. He likes to think of it as 'The Click', when they know, when the process becomes open and a line is formed from question to answer. He once lived for those moments. They were wonderful: frustration to enlightenment. But since she left, whirlwind, taking the air with her, he has taught Math without passion and the life of numbers has faded. The lessons are presented, tests are given, and judgment is pronounced. But the victories no longer hold meaning and the faces run together, melding into one child, into one face: a dull, lifeless thing.

Henry strides through the hallways, looking over the tops of young heads, as they struggle between innocent childhood and innocent adulthood. The chatter of young voices fills the space, high-pitched wails of young girls and young boys. It almost makes Henry smile. Several students greet him and look up at him.

"Hello, Mr. Kent."

He nods, bigger than them, stronger, helpful model of what to be in years to come. They are the future, part of a larger whole, great beyond their knowledge of self or society, greater still because of their potential. And they are the greatest disappointment because they will squander all the gifts of youth. Henry reaches out briefly to the pain of the hall, the lament at the future and then quickly enters the faculty lounge.

"That motherfucker." The voice is loud and angry. Henry smiles and takes his place at the long table that dominates the room. There is also a couch, a computer with a chimpanzee screen saver, posters decorate the walls and the coffee maker is always on.

The occupants include Jon Smith, Science teacher, Hal Allen, History, and the loudest of them all Barry Jordan, English, who continues to rant.

"She fucking said that about my scores."

Henry leans forward and speaks to Hal, "What's he on about?"

"Principal said his scores on the Eighth Grade Exam were too low," Hal responds sipping his coffee.

"Oh."

"Yeah," Barry continues. "She fucking told me I'd better get the kids to perform better on the spring assessment."

Henry mixes his coffee, watching Barry. The English teacher is close to retirement, but not close enough, five years away, five long years. He's been a hyperactive man since Henry has known him, bouncing here and there, concerned about his position and getting his full time.

"The fucking kids are dumb. I can't work with Ritalin addicted twelve-year-olds. What do they want from me?"

Henry knows Barry's anxiety, his need to be thought of as strong and dedicated. His mannerisms, deconstructed, show his fear of the world, his irrational apprehension of reality. He covets the world of school and renounces it, wants it to mean something but knows he's forgotten in time as children grow to become adults. Henry takes his coffee and leaves.

Episode 4: Touch of Evil

Henry is assigned hall duty during his free period in the morning. He enjoys the solitude of the duty, the stillness of the world. The halls are usually very quiet between classes, focused energy wrapped in growing limbs, adolescent angst at the unsure world, not yet defined, still a child's dream and a teenager's dread. Henry wanders the halls, absent of pain and the pangs of terror. He strolls slowly, sipping his coffee, thinking of her. She left, like his mother, perhaps like all women, gone on a whim, and poor Arthur. He wants to hate her, to despise her, an excuse for self-pity and to try again with another one, to start over. A strange noise emanating from the boy's lavatory catches his attention and he goes to investigate.

He comes upon a scene of a boy holding another boy down, sitting on his chest and pining his arms above his head. The victim is smaller than his attacker, helpless and petrified, caught as animal would be. The other boy has a look of glee on his face, a sadist at a young age.

"Don't yell. Don't you fucking yell again." The attacker's voice is hushed, seething through his teeth. "This is going to hurt."

Henry watches, frozen momentarily by the mature violence of the situation, the ferocity and the coldness. But duty compensates.

"What's going on here?" His voice fills the bathroom. The innocent looks up, relieved, saved.

The sadist turns, unafraid. He moves slowly and releases his captive. The smaller child runs behind the teacher. "I asked you a question," Henry tells the attacker, who is dressed well, collared shirt, clean pants, styled hair. He's not overly large, average for his age, nothing distinguishable, nothing announcing his savagery.

"We were only playing." The words are not rushed or forced.

Henry smiles. Bullies need boundaries, right and wrong. He was part of a seminar about curbing violence in schools, even played golf in the annual tournament to raise awareness.

"Is that so?" Henry's voice takes on the air of superiority. Diana hated the voice. She always stormed off and refused to continue the discussion when he used it.

"Yes, Mr. Kent."

Henry nods and looks at the smaller child. "Is that the truth, young man?"

The child's head is bent down, staring at his sneakers. He's small, perhaps a pituitary deficiency, something keeping him from growing and fighting back. His pain is obvious. Henry can taste it. The all-encompassing agony of the situation fills Henry and he shudders. The pervasiveness of the torment hangs in the air. This is not the first time, not even the second or the third. He's almost used to it by now, but never really used to it. Always a shock, always painful, always the afterward, the imagination, the sense of doom each day, knowing he's watching and plotting it again. It's enough to make someone stop and fade away to numbness, to nothingness. Henry wants to hold the boy, become the avenger, the protector, Superman to an eleven-year-old.

"Uhhhh…"

Henry glances again at the attacker. The boy has moved backward, closer to the window, hiding in the gray light of winter. The child seems confident, looking through the teacher into his victim, controlling him. Henry wants to hurt the bully, break his neck and drop him out the window or leave him in a stall, upside down with his head in a toilet.

"…uhhh, yeah."

Henry turns. The innocent's head is still down, eyes still on the floor, backing away.

"Is that…"

The innocent small thing, precious in the world, walks slowly to the exit. Henry cannot stop him and the child disappears out the door.

The attacker, the confident fiend walks to the teacher.

"Don't let me catch you again." Henry attempts to grow larger, threatening.

"Yes, you won't catch me again." The boy brushes past him.

Henry clenches his fist, cocks his arm, comes close, so very close, but the boy is gone. The teacher moves to follow him, prove to him that authority exists in the world and that the wicked are punished. The boy would cower. Henry would show him that atrocities will not be tolerated. But a gleam on the floor distracts his attention. He kneels before the puddle of urine, a damp stain on the green linoleum. The ghosts of terror are still pungent and Henry shivers.

Episode 5: Picture the World as You Like

Arthur attends a special school. He waits stoically outside the building, bundled up, in the softly falling snow. His scarf, which is blue with horizontal stripes, is wrapped around his mouth twice. The other children, more severe and less affected by the world, remain in the building watching through fogged windows. Arthur cannot wait inside, the brown room, solid colors, and no movement. He is compelled to stand outside amongst the wind and the cold on the sidewalk, two feet from the curb, cleared of snow for him. His breath turns to white mist, almost measured in time and energy.

Henry appears in the SUV, a wake of open space behind him. Arthur is handed a towel and boards the vehicle. The boy wipes his boots clean, no remnants of snow, careful in each movement. The towel is placed in a plastic bag and put on the back seat. The radio plays the news, always a voice, the pitch, the resonance, the obvious meaning, no mystery in syntax or connotation.

"Did you bring the camera?" Arthur asks in a quiet voice. He is usually silent after school, processing the day's events, categorizing and analyzing.

"Yes," Henry answers.

"Could we drive for a while?"

24

"Sure."

Henry hands his son the digital camera and drives the established route. He watches Arthur take pictures as scenery floats by and a more persistent snow falls. Today must have been trying for Arthur, unpredictable. Henry remembers a note announcing a Christmas party, different food and a visit from Santa.

He also remembers his wife was wary of their drives after school and the need for pictures. The conversations between son and mother were often tedious.

"Is that a good one," Diana would ask.

"No," Arthur would respond.

"How come?"

"Just isn't."

"How can you tell?" she would ask, watching her son closely.

"I can. I just can," Arthur would answer.

"Okay," Diana would say.

"There's something different about you," Arthur said once.

"Oh."

"New perfume?"

"Maybe."

"Why?"

"Just something different," Diana responded.

"Why?" Arthur asked.

"I needed a change."

"Why?"

"Why anything?"

"Because there's always a why."

"Sometimes there's nothing," Diana said.

"Why?" Arthur asked.

"It's the way of the world."

"Why?"

"I don't know."

"That's not good enough," Arthur said very seriously.

"Not knowing is fine. No one knows everything," Diana said with a smile.

"Why?"

"Again, my love, it's the way of the world."

"Not my world."

"No, you're special."

"Why is that?" Arthur asked.

"Because someone has to be," his mother told him.

And then she was gone, when her son no longer proved amusing. When she no longer could answer his questions, when 'I don't know' was true and all knowledge was lost and then she was gone.

Arthur never questioned her departure or even commented on the absence of his mother. The routine of his life rolled past the missing person as if she was never that important. There are times when Henry questions his own necessity in his son's life. His duties are important. His role as cook, chauffeur, sounding board are intricate, but his actual person, father, friend seem inconsequential. Arthur's world spins in this beauty. Henry is envious at times, jealous of the single-minded nature of his son, dedicated to trivia and his own monumentally important needs. His son thrives in this world of cemented rules and procedures. The next thing will happen, things will fall into place or else the world will end.

Arthur watches the snow, looking through the flakes, unlocking the mystery of it all. The car slows and a picture is taken: older woman walking her dog. It's easier in the summer, more people, but it must be all year, a relief, a release, preserving the sanity of the world. Henry drives carefully, slowing when he senses Arthur's want for a photograph. The ride comes to an end in an hour's time.

At home Arthur disappears into the basement, his basement, his universe. Henry begins dinner. He will make something appropriate for his son, what is required for a Monday. Eventually Henry descends to find Arthur well into his work.

The tables take up the majority of the room. Folding tables bought at a garage sale, a picnic table, pieces of plywood on two sawhorses, variations of each spread over the room, different heights, lengths, yet all connected. They're covered with pictures, cut and placed in holders standing amongst toy cars, models, pictures of buildings, milk cartons; a thousand inhabitants of an eclectic city landscape, random and exact. Arthur prints the pictures from his camera. The computer needed to be relocated for the task. He shrinks the images, makes his own stands from paperclips and places the new citizens within the confines of the ever-growing city.

Arthur controls the populace with a gentle, yet realistic hand. He is aware, even at his tender age, that people die or simply disappear. He knows that there is great darkness in the world. He has created slums, populated by seedy characters and those who dream of one day escaping poverty. The affluent neighborhood is littered with hollow men and women, burnt out by success and the excesses of life. There are mysteries in the city, known only to the creator. It all melds together, intricate and divine.

Henry watches his son go about the task of minding his creation. Soon a new table will be needed, over by the river that empties somewhere beyond the boundaries of Arthur's creation. New citizens are processed, given stories and histories and placed within their new home. Some are moved, some are born, some die, some achieve and some fail.

"Who's that, Arthur?"

The child looks up, hovering over the industrial area, pictures of an abandoned steel plant and polluted ponds, a wasteland east of the city. "This? This is Mrs. Grayson. She's looking for her son. He disappeared a month ago. She's worried. He has a history of trouble. It comes from her, she thinks. She was never stable. Her son saw things. They might have made him crazy. He's that kind of boy. He follows his whims."

"Do you know what happened to him?" Henry asks.

"Yes."

"Can you tell me?"

"Not yet. Mrs. Grayson will want to find out for herself. Finding out will make her happy. Even if he's dead, she'll want to know. She'll feel like she's done something for her son."

"Is he dead?"

"I can't tell you. It's a secret. It would ruin everything if everyone knew what was going to happen. That's why Mrs. Grayson is here. The search will give her something to do." Arthur almost smiles. "Something to do."

Henry glances at the city, the sprawling, living thing, built on fantasy and reality; a world of ingenuity, born of a fevered brain. Arthur moves over his creation, deciding life and death, oblivion and peace, how it will all work out in the end. Henry's son focuses all his will into thousands of other wills and almost smiles.

"Dinner will be ready soon."

"Fifteen minutes," Arthur replies.

"Yes."

Henry walks around the city, the perimeter of the world. He looks at the faces of strangers. Alien eyes stare back, except, very quickly, in the alley, part of a small group, Diana. Beautiful Diana is part of the world, standing among a throng of people looking at something. The picture is from a picnic, years ago, younger Diana, haunting Diana. She had long hair then, past her shoulders, smooth face, pristine, perfect. Henry is at once there with her, happy to be a picture, living under the watchful eye of a known god.

"Arthur…"

"I can't tell you, Dad."

Henry looks to his son and watches him place a building in an empty space, another apartment complex, more people coming, a home for everyone except the homeless. Henry reaches toward the picture of his wife.

"Dad, please don't touch."

"Arthur, your mother…"

"Yes."

"Arthur…"

"She has to be somewhere."

Henry retracts his hand, takes another quick look and walks upstairs to finish preparing dinner.

Epilogue to Episode 5: Henry's Dream

Diana was a wonderful small action figure, five inches tall, articulated at all the proper joints, capable of thought and independent movement. Henry took her out the package and sat her down among the other action figures, superheroes, GI Joe, male dolls all. He watched as they moved about her, admiring her form. He set up dates between several male figures and his wife and watched with triumph as she denied each advance. She gazed lovingly up at the hand that controlled the world. He reached down and picked her up, she smiled, plastic lips and teeth. With a swift motion he tore her head off and smashed the toy to the ground. There was no blood. He placed the pieces in the trashcan. He went to the local store and bought another Diana figure and played the game again.

Episode 6: The Horizon Doesn't End

It's the first decisively cold day of the year. There is no hint of fall or anticipation for spring. December has changed finally and it's the death of warm breezes. The snow has accumulated over night, deepening the life of the world. The air is clean, hurtful in his lungs, a reminder that pain is present in stages, agonies that are monumental and slight, cold air in the lungs and the death of the world. Henry clenches as he walks to his school. The building is dark in the morning, dark in the evening, permanent twilight and pitch now, living without the sun for months. He wraps his coat about him and pulls his gloves tight. It's hard to relax, to stretch himself, to feel the world spin. Head down, eyes narrowed, fighting the wind, he trudges through the snow that crunches under foot.

The morning rituals proceed without pause. Announcements are read and children scurry to and fro. Christmas is coming. Decorations line the walls, frivolity in the light of every day dangers. It's only been one year since a child was killed in a school shooting in the neighboring district. Henry knew the family, played golf with Sam Jafar and hugged him when his son was buried. There was also a hero, the principal who paid the hero's price for his bravery. It was an important event, rattling the small suburbs.

Henry pushes any sense of gloom from his mind and concentrates on quadratic formulas with his advanced class. Children crave learning and Henry needs their enthusiasm. He knows that most will not be able to maintain such energy and will succumb to the pressures of adolescence. But here, he tells himself, they care and that's enough.

The faculty room is quiet as Henry enters. A strong wind rattles the windows.

"It's going to snow for another hour." The voice is hushed. The origin is Oliver Lance, veteran teacher of more than thirty years. He has a reputation for being difficult, eccentric, and a genius. Rumors circle about him involving a wonderful narrative full of passion, disgrace, ultimate failure and empty potential, but he's only a Math teacher in the end. Still, as Henry started his career, Mr. Lance was a suspicious person of interest. Over the six years Henry has been teaching, Mr. Lance has seemingly taken a liking to him.

"What's that, Ollie?"

"It's going to snow for another hour."

"Is that so?"

"Yes."

Henry nods and smiles. Mr. Lance says many things, precise things, exact things. Colleagues laugh at him behind his back, think less of him. He's rarely wrong.

"How have you been, Hank?"

Henry sits at the rectangle table, a box of donuts is open in the middle and the smell of coffee hangs in the air. Henry picks a powdered donut. "Not too bad. Can't complain."

Mr. Lance sips from a cup without symbol or picture. "Any word from Diana?"

"No, not in a while." Henry stands, pours a cup of coffee and stirs in cream. He has a passing memory of a Christmas party when Diana called Mr. Lance 'intense, but in an interesting way.'

"And how is Arthur doing with all this?"

"Fine, I suppose. He doesn't talk much. I'm sure he knows something is wrong."

"Yes, things are changing."

"World has to spin."

"Perhaps and perhaps not."

"How are you, Ollie? Haven't seen you in here in a while. How did your little sabbatical go?"

"Fine." Mr. Lance sips from his cup, adjusts his tie, and cleans his glasses. "I was working on something and needed the time, as I told you."

"Yes, but you didn't tell me what you were working on. There's all sorts of speculation."

Mr. Lance pauses and leans closer to Henry. He speaks in a guarded tone. "Things are changing, Hank. I've watched you since you started here. You know what I'm talking about. You can't put your finger on it, with all that's happening, but you know."

"Ollie, I can pretend that makes sense, but honestly I'm not sure."

"Yes, no one is sure, no one."

"Things are always changing, everything moves forward, you've said that before. I thought you were getting help."

"Yes, yes." Mr. Lance sits back and looks out the window. Snow is still falling, sideways and slanted as a strong wind blows. "Forward and inevitable."

Henry watches him, the older teacher, now teaching grandchildren of children.

"Hank, I have something to tell you. It's important."

"Are you still getting that help? Did you stop going?" Henry asks.

"No, I mean yes. It's not that simple. This is far beyond any of that."

The door opens abruptly. Jordan and Allen walk in, laughing. Mr. Lance retracts, almost afraid. Allen and Jordan sit. They speak of sports and politics. Mr. Lance watches them and Henry watches Mr. Lance. The old man rises in time and moves toward the exit. He nods to Henry who looks blankly at his mentor. The door closes without a sound.

"What were you two doing?" asks Jordan.

"Nothing. Don't be a prick," Henry responds.

"Hank, you know that old coot is fucking crazy. This job is all he has. Shit his wife up and left, when was it? Like a decade ago," Jordan announces.

"Disappeared," Allen whispers.

"Yeah. One minute she's there and the next, gone. And he doesn't talk about it."

"Sometimes it's best to keep personal problems personal," Henry responds.

Allen interjects, "Hank, we're teachers. There's nothing we don't know. There's no problem we can't solve."

"Maybe he misses her and doesn't want to talk about her because it hurts," Henry says as he drinks his coffee.

"Lance is a strange fucker," Jordan announces. "He was supposed to be close with the principal who was shot last year."

"The hero?" Henry asks.

"Yeah, big news last year and now, no one gives a shit. Guy gets shot, saves lives and they're trying to fuck us in the contract. I tell ya, you can't do enough. It's always about numbers and the last article in the paper. Not even getting shot satisfies them."

"He's got another meeting about his grades and they want to see his lesson plans," Allen tells Henry.

"Fuck them," Jordan concludes.

Allen opens the newspaper. Jordan paces the room, building to something. Henry finishes his donut.

Allen looks up from the paper. "Did you see several soldiers died yesterday in a car bombing? It was all over the news last night."

Jordan welcomes the change in topic. "There's supposed to be another major attack. Guy on the radio this

33

morning said there was good evidence that something is going to happen soon. Whole world's going to hell."

Allen folds the paper. "Even in our little school. Did you hear that one of our lovelies was attacked last night?"

"What?" Henry asks, interested.

"One of the secretaries in the main office told me. Robert Kanjar had the shit beat out him."

Jordan asks, "What happened?"

"Did you know him?" Allen asks.

"No, not really. Only by reputation."

"You know him, Hank?"

"Only like Barry, by reputation."

Allen continues, "He's a fucker, that one. He's mouthed off to several teachers, couple of fights, suspended numerous times. I guess when they found him he had a knife and some prescription pills. They found some more in his locker."

"So what about the ass-kicking?" Jordan asks.

"Well, there's not much detail about the specifics. Kid is in the hospital with broken ribs, broken nose. I guess he's really messed up. They think it's drug related. Hell the little bastard should be a sophomore in high school instead of the eighth grade."

"Like I said, the world's going to hell."

Henry looks out the window. The snow has stopped falling.

Prologue to Episode 7

Never liked thin snow, too light, like dust.

It's time for more than simply watching. No need to take them all on at once. Better this way. Make them spread the story. Make them afraid.

That one. Stronger than the rest. No remorse. No conscience. No redeeming quality. Good and evil. Truth and justice. A hero must do what a hero must. They stalk the earth, stalk the innocent…the fearful…the small…and they feel big. They're not children, not anymore.

A hero has a choice to make, be benevolent, never killing, but even Superman killed. Or the other type, death from above, out of the shadows, righteous vengeance. Time to take that next step.

He's trailing behind, the big one. He's curious about the snow, the aesthetic quality of the white world. He'll remember this. He'll change after this. Take him now, strike from the shadows. Won't kill him, not yet, not yet. There's still time. There's still hope.

Episode 7: One Man's Crime...

Arthur is up earlier than normal, two minutes. Startled, his father finds him at the table.

"Arthur. Is everything all right?"

"Yes... no. I'm not sure." The boy sits at the table in his pajamas, elephants at the circus. There is a glass of orange juice on the table.

"Do you need your medication?"

"I don't think so. No, I don't." He sips the orange juice.

"I'll start breakfast."

"Yes, that's it, breakfast. I was thinking... and it's breakfast."

Arthur continues to sit quietly, gazing out the window. The remnants of last night's snow flutter down, resting on the ground.

"It snowed last night. It wasn't much, but another inch," Arthur says.

"Yes it did."

"There's now three feet of snow... in the areas where it's allowed to collect."

"Yes."

"That's a two foot difference from last year. Different from yesterday too. And tomorrow it might be different again or it might be the same. Hard to tell now. Sky is gray. It might snow and it might not. Hard to tell what will happen."

"Did you have trouble sleeping last night?" Henry asks as the sausage sizzles and a bagel pops from the toaster.

"Yes, a little bit. Not sure why, not sure why it was different. But you're right. It was different and it will take time to adjust. Maybe a day, maybe less."

"Breakfast."

Henry places the plate before his son: half a bagel, top half, two sausage links and one egg scrambled with two twists of pepper. Arthur eats cautiously. After breakfast Henry and his son dress for school.

Henry can feel the cold of winter pushing on the house, as the world settles in for months of tension, wrapping itself in snow and ice. Diana liked the winter; she talked of snow as if it were a person, capable of great things.

"See how it twirls in the air, dancing in the sky between the ground and heaven. Isn't it beautiful?" she would say.

"You're beautiful," Henry would respond.

"Stop that, I'm trying to tell you something." She would smile at him. "Watch the snow and the wind. See how the flakes leap off the ground. There are times when you can't tell if the snow is rising or falling. I like those times. They're rare though. And you have to catch them just right."

"Your eyes are beautiful," Henry would tell her.

"I was a dancer, you know? I danced ballet for a while, when I was young. I stopped though. I knew I wouldn't be good enough so I stopped. It was important to me. It was my life for a time. It's hard to give that sort of thing up. It leaves you empty in a way."

"You're still beautiful."

Henry watches the snow fall from his bedroom window, where Diana once sat and watched the snow. It falls gently, piling up on the lawn near the deck. After a moment he goes to find Arthur.

His son is in the basement minding his city, moving pieces here and there. The boy's appearance seems off. Henry can't quite grasp what is wrong, but there is something, a lack of smoothness to Arthur's movements.

"How are the citizens today?" Henry asks.

"Restless."

"Yes, so it seems."

"There was a storm last night. Thunder and lightning swept the city. Giant raindrops fell. Several buildings were damaged. Some people died."

"That's a shame."

"People die."

Henry paces the tables, looking at the faces, looking for her face. She is no longer in the alley. He scans the faces again, morning rush hour, cars and traffic, voices over the roar of the city.

"Arthur, where's-"

"I can't tell you, Dad. She has a life and it doesn't pause or stop. She's fine though. I can tell you that."

"I guess that's good enough."

"Yes."

"And how's Mrs. Grayson?"

"The storm frightened her. She didn't sleep last night. She blames it on the hotel room, strange bed, different sheets. But she's always been afraid of the thunder and the lightning. She's drinking coffee now."

"And her son?"

"Nothing yet. But at least it's daytime. At least the storm is over."

Henry nods and continues to circle the tables. Arthur folds another paperclip and the new resident is put in his spot, on top of a tall building.

"Who's that? I thought you deleted the rest of the pictures from yesterday."

"This? This is someone special. I've been saving this one."

Henry walks over to the new citizen.

"It's getting late, Dad. We should go. There's another party today. There'll be cupcakes and orange drink. I'll have to eat some. I'm not sure if Santa is coming back. But I think there's another special person coming to school today."

"Okay, Arthur. We are running a bit behind." Henry glances at the city again, to the building and he recognizes the new member of the population. "Who is that?"

"A hero, I think," Arthur responds while putting on his scarf.

"It looks like... like..."

"That principal that saved all those kids last year. I downloaded a picture of him before he was shot. He has his own website. I've been saving it until it was needed."

"Why now?"

"He has work to do."

"Why is he on top of that building?"

"He wants to see the city as it should be."

"What's he going to do?"

"That would be telling."

Arthur's face disappears behind his scarf. But right before his mouth is lost, Henry sees it, faintly, quickly, almost a smile.

Henry is usually the first to arrive at school, a tradeoff for Arthur not having to take the bus. Henry's school is always dark when he arrives, dark against the gray sky. He stops and looks about, alone in the gloom, a tainted darkness. The cold comes on the wind, through his coat, touching his skin. He stands against it until another car appears, the headlights highlighting individual snowflakes. He clenches and enters the school.

The morning classes proceed without incident: equations to answer, problems with solutions, some frustration, and a smile. Henry's motions are mechanical, the same jokes as last class, the same lessons, the ebb and flow of another year. Henry enters the faculty room and pours a cup of coffee. Allen and Jordan soon follow. Allen drops a box of donuts on the table.

"How was your meeting, Barry?" Henry asks.

"I had to bring Allen with me as my union rep. You know how O'Brien can be."

"Yeah."

"I'm supposed to go to this fucking reeducation program."

"Are you going to go?"

"Fuck that. If it's not in the contract, I'm not required to attend."

"So now what?"

"Nothing. Life goes on. I keep telling myself five more years. All I have to do is get through five more years."

"That's rough."

"Five years."

"What about the kids that failed the test?" Henry asks as he takes a glazed donut from the box.

"What about them?" Jordan asks.

Allen sits next to Henry and asks, "Hey, did you hear about the fight yesterday?"

Henry stares at Jordan for a moment, watching the man as he stares at his coffee as if he might be lost in it and then turns to Allen. "No."

"Well, I guess fight isn't the right word. A seventh grader was found in the lavatory. Poor kid was naked. Someone duct-taped him to the stall."

"In the lav?" Henry remembers the stain on the floor.

"Yeah, I guess the kid's a mess now. Two incidents in two days."

"World's going to hell," Jordan announces as he looks for a jelly donut.

"What was the kid's name?" Henry asks.

"Ronald Digby. Nice kid. I have him in class. Quiet."

Henry's hand trembles slightly. He makes a fist. "Do they know who did it?"

"No clue." Allen sips his coffee. "Nothing's happened like this in a couple of years. Remember that seminar on violence? That presenter was hot."

"Yeah. But the rest of it was a waste of time. Half these kids are animals when they get to school," Jordan concludes as he finishes his donut, wiping the excess jelly from his chin.

"Which bathroom was it?" Henry pushes the remainder of his donut away.

"This hallway. They found the Digby kid at the end of the day. Custodian cleaning up. I guess the poor kid was almost unconscious. I suppose there'll be an investigation. Ah hell, they didn't give me any chocolate ones." Allen makes do with a cruller. "O'Brien wants to have a meeting today to discuss the bullying. Try to pinpoint the exact time of the incident. Parents are already talking lawsuit."

"Why wouldn't they?" Henry answers, angry.

Jordan looks out the window, his eyes following the snowflakes as they fall. "What are you talkin' about, Hank?" he asks.

"We can't protect the kids from each other. What are we doing if we can't even keep them safe in school? They should be safe here." Henry grows more reflective. "We have little psychotics running around in the halls. We know who will be good and who won't. I see it everyday, but we don't do anything. No one does anything. We just let it go. Someone else will catch them. Eventually they'll pay. We know that most of these kids are set in their lives. They are who they are. They're not going to change that much. They're only going to get worse, through high school, through college, if they get there. It should be here. Here we could still help them… save them."

Jordan leans over the table. "Jesus, Hank, still not getting any?"

Allen shakes his head. Henry looks quickly to Jordan, his power washing over the English Teacher.

He's a broken man in a frayed shirt, holding on to this job he hates, self-loathing and weak. He'll kill himself a year after retirement and leave only pornography and an unfinished novel behind.

Henry stands and leaves.

Allen looks at Jordan. "You're such an asshole."

"What?" Jordan responds as he hunts for another donut.

41

Episode 8: …Is Another Man's Cause

The lavatory is placid when classes are in session. The only sounds are the soft hum of the lights and the dripping of the faucets. The sole window is tinted as to give no clue of the outside world. The stalls are a thin metal and the doors are open at strange angles. Henry touches one, sticky still, remnants of duct-tape. The toilets are small, miniature for pseudo-people playing at adulthood. It smells like a bathroom, strong deodorant hangs in the air, fighting the scents of preteen sweat and excrement.

Henry's hand remains on the stall with the scars of tape. He closes his eyes and reaches out with his power, reaches back in time to the terror, to the all-encompassing fear that this is it, this is the end. No one to save you now. No one to come to your rescue. This is the worst. This will never leave you. This will be part of you forever. Years and years from now, when you're an adult with a family, pretty wife, in bed, you'll remember this in the shadows of your bedroom, a ghost, a tangible phantom and you'll cry. You might be a strong man with a powerful job, but everything you might have built will be meaningless and you'll whimper quietly, thinking of this. This will be your life, this one terrible thing will be all you are and I'll have done that. You'll remember how I exposed your skin to the cold metal, how I put that last piece of tape over your mouth. Your pleas were meaningless sounds. You saw that I knew all this. I knew exactly what I was doing and I didn't care. Because I'll do worse than this. You're nothing, a waste of time. This is the world to you and a joke to me.

Henry's hand falters. He stumbles to the window and opens it. A gust of wind pushes him back. The snow is rising from the ground, lifted by hands of wind. Henry touches the window frame, ice and metal. This winter will be brutal, the unforgiving cold will last and the ice will leave deep scars.

A bell rings and voices fill the void. The door opens and children pause when they see a teacher.

"Mr. Kent…"

"Hello, Mr. Kent…"

"Mr. Kent…"

Henry turns and walks past them, holding his power in, afraid, unwilling to know them. He falls into the hallway, as startled students stare. Henry takes a second to compose himself and smiles at the passing faces. Above them to the right he sees a child, the child from Monday, cruel child, evil child. The noise dies down, the hall grows calm and there is only the hero and the villain.

"Mr. Kent, you're going to be late."

A tugging at his arm and the halls live again. He looks down and there is a small girl smiling at him. He sees his reflection in her thick glasses. She's in his next class. He walks with her, looking back once.

Henry enters the main office and is greeted by the three secretaries who make the school run smoothly. They have always liked Henry for some reason, his boyish looks or the fact he's always been overly polite with them, as his mother taught him or the fact they're all mothers and they know his son is different. One secretary in particular, the oldest, the most knowledgeable of the school has always been particularly friendly with him. Her name is Dinah. Henry sees his grandmother in her face, his father's mother, pleasant, knowing many things but only revealing what she needs to. She's dressed in a festive sweater, Santa Claus and reindeer, very bright and cheerful. She touches Henry's arm and asks about Arthur. She dresses a certain way and asks certain questions because she's supposed to, it's expected of her and she does what is expected of her when she's with people she doesn't trust.

"He's fine," Henry responds smiling.

"I bet he's excited for Christmas," Dinah says, almost glowing with merriment.

"As excited as he gets." They share a brief grin and Henry changes the subject. "Do you know anything about what happened yesterday?"

"The boy in the bathroom? Digby?"

"Yes."

"Terrible thing, that. I don't know much. I do know Digby is withdrawing from school."

"Any word on who did it?"

"No, nothing." She pauses and glances at her shoes. "It's terrible."

Henry watches her. He touches her on the shoulder. She looks up and forces a smile. Henry asks, "Is O'Brien in?"

"Yes. She's not with anyone if you need to talk to her." The secretary's face loses some its glow and she sits down and looks at her computer.

Henry pauses before O'Brien's door, then knocks and enters. The principal is seated at her desk. She doesn't have a first name, doesn't need it, simply O'Brien: principal, bitch, queen cunt and the other titles she's been given filter about her. She's young for her position and smart, perhaps too smart. She came from a private school, the best private school. Henry's school was lucky to get her. Most of the teachers hate her, too sure of herself, sure of the world. Arrogant skank, pushy dyke:

O'Brien. She's sitting with her head down, focused on her computer. She looks up when Henry coughs, but she is expressionless, lost in something else.

"O'Brien."

"Hello, Henry." She returns to her computer screen. "I'll be with you in a minute. Have a seat."

Henry sits and looks about the office. It seems in turmoil, odd deviation from the norm.

"What can I do for you, Henry?"

"It's about the boy who was attacked yesterday."

"Yes?"

"I think I may know who did it. That is, if it was the same boy."

"Come again?"

"I stopped a fight yesterday in the bathroom, the same bathroom. Two boys. I think it may be the same boy who was attacked."

"I think I have a good idea who did it."

"You do?"

"I can't do anything. No proof. In fact the Digbys called and asked I forget the whole situation. They're taking their son out of school. They said it would be safer than-"

"You have to do something," Henry interjects and leans forward.

"I know. It's spreading around the school. The violence. It's changing people."

"Who did it? What's the boy's name?"

"I can't tell you."

"I can find out."

"Yes, Henry, you can."

"This isn't right."

"No it isn't. It's wrong and horrible and a crime. This is a sign of things to come. It's a reflection of the way things are."

"O'Brien, we have to-"

"You know, Henry, people feel safe and need that; to feel safe. Basic Maslow, right? Safety first." Henry watches O'Brien and there's something different in her, some change that he cannot understand. "We build paper walls of protection and then a wind comes, a cold wind and everything is blown away. And we're left as we truly are, exposed and scared. The world is a dark place and all we can do is protect the ones we love. Can't do anything else, not really. We lie and tell ourselves we're safe. We lie to our children because we want so desperately to protect them. But there are dangers in the world and everything won't be all right."

"O'Brien, is there something else? Something…"

"Henry?" She seems surprised suddenly. "No. There is nothing else to do, nothing at all to do." She pauses. "Is there anything else you wanted?"

Henry stands, unsure, afraid to reach out, yet there is something there. "No." He leaves.

The secretaries are quiet in the outer office, bustling about the day's business. Henry stops in front of the one who reminds him of his grandmother.

"Hey Dinah, is everything all right with O'Brien?"

"I think so. Rough day. Lots of phone calls. She was talking to that one kid for an hour."

"What kid?"

"I forget his name. Nice looking, well dressed. Like I said after talking to him she hasn't been out of her office all day."

"Thanks, Dinah."

Episode 9: The Ominous Days Before

He's still looking around, scanning for a possible escape. Looking at me too, watching me. He blinks quickly, blood from the cut on his forehead dripping into his eyes.

The physique of the hero is crucial. Beyond the need to be able to do the impossible physically, acrobat, one-punch knockout, martial arts, and all the things the hero must do in the physical world, the image presented is all-important. End the fight by being bigger. Intimidation under the spandex and the body-armor. 'Don't fight me, because you'll lose and it'll hurt when you do.' Hours spent lifting, running, training for the moment when the hero must be more than his or her opponent. Unless, of course the hero is somehow enhanced, strength of a spider, alien, nuclear, power bolts from the hands. These heroes are then intimidating because of their closeness to divinity and cannot be in the same category as your average 'human' hero. But where as these powerful, godlike heroes thwart alien invasions and disasters on a biblical scale, the lone ordinary hero fights on a smaller, more intimate scale when intimidation is put to use in an alley or on a rooftop or in a warehouse. And because they are human, prone to faults associated with humanity, their actions can be erratic, their motives often dark, their results ultimately a grand failure.

47

He's flinching when the bat comes close, preparing himself for the pain. There's something to that.

The day ends with the mysteries of factoring a binomial. The children feel different. A cloud hangs about them, just above their heads, without form, a mirror of the sky beyond the school. Henry stands in it and breathes the fear, the trepidation, the fundamental shift of each life, danger is near and the night is full of monsters. Eventually the final bell sounds and the children filter out into the world.

She came in quietly, while his head was down, focused on a quiz, a wrong answer, the process flawed somewhere. She slipped in, back of the room, and is watching him. He concentrates on the paper, following the line of thought, each step leads to another, but somewhere little Johnny Jones, second seat middle row, third period, made an error and reached the wrong outcome. One slip, one number mishandled and the end is wrong. Maybe he was distracted by something, homework and television and he missed the secret code, the answer that makes everything the way it's supposed to be. Henry concentrates, fix the mistake with red ink, show the error and learn from it and move forward. And it's there, the error, simple addition, one off, simple and the answer is correct.

Henry looks up but does not react right away. It's as if he expected to see her, she should just be there. He leans back slightly and watches her in the dull light of early twilight. She seems the same, as she's always been.

"Mr. Kent," a high voice speaks.

Henry looks to the door.

"Do you think we'll get a snow day tomorrow?" little Johnny Jones asks with a smile.

"I hope so. See you."

"Bye, Mr. Kent."

He pauses before looking back at her. It might have been nothing before, might be nothing still. He looks and she smiles. She's in shadow, the lights turned off save for the bank above Henry's desk, but he knows she's smiling. His eyes fall back to his desk, numbers and equations.

"Are you going to say something?"

Henry remembers a dream. She was beautiful in the dream, a fragile porcelain doll. He held her loosely, as if she might break all to pieces. He tried to drink her in, her skin, her hair, the great dark pools of her eyes. He woke up late that morning, wanting to stay in the dream.

"Henry, won't you say something?"

The numbers are still there, fixed on the papers, etched in black pencil. He pictures her, sitting in the small desk, uncomfortable.

"You came back?" Henry asks.

"I did."

"Hmm."

"I did."

The wind pushes on the frozen window, which creaks, metal and glass. The sun peaks out and the ice becomes a web of crystal.

"Why?"

"I suppose I had nothing else to do."

Henry looks up, red pen in hand.

"That's cruel. I'm sorry. I can't tell you yet," she says. "I'm not ready to explain everything yet. Let it be a mystery for a while. It's better that way. If I told you now, I'd have to leave again and come back again."

Henry leans back and rests his head on the blackboard. "You have to say something. I want to hear you say something," he tells her.

"Shall I quote someone or paraphrase something?"

"As you like."

She remains in the shadows, pacing along the back wall.

"It was a little revolution," she begins. "A revolution that fizzled, as those things have a tendency to do. I thought I was doing something, finally living, to a manner of speaking. More of a rebellion than a revolution."

"Against what?"

"Pardon?"

"What were you rebelling against? Was it like James Dean and you were looking for something? Or was it something different like a grand, futile gesture?"

"You always were smart. You're really nothing like your dad. I hope you didn't compare yourself to him when I was gone. But, I suppose you must have. You're not like him, though. You never were."

Henry glances at the clock. Time is marching forward. He thinks of Mr. Lance. "I have to get Arthur."

"Arthur." She stops pacing near the window. Her face is ashen, reflecting the light. "Should I keep talking?"

"Yes."

"I could continue about revolutions, personal ones that peter out."

Henry puts on his coat. "Is that why you left?"

"Maybe. Maybe not. We should go. Arthur will be upset if we're late."

Episode 10: The War in All People

He's scared, but not of what he should be. He scared because he's exposed. Tied to the chair, the twine cutting into his skin.

The villain's appearance is tied to and in most cases reflects the nature of the event that made the villain villainous. Scarred or disfigured, raging against society that does not accept the change, the villain may choose ridiculous attire, flaunting their alienation from accepted society. Thus do they show themselves different and accentuate the fact that the bonds of society no longer constrain them. The attire then becomes a statement and an identity. Of course this is the case of the non-psychotic, non-homicidal villain. This example is of those tragic villains, who through circumstances are forced to become outsiders, whether they are villains or not.

Now as to the other type of villain, they fall into either of two categories. The first type is the god-like like characters, often shown as dark aspects of fundamental forces. Iconic in appearance, they strive for some unmaking of the universe. And subsequently their appearance is awe-inspiring and beyond the normal human understanding. And since they look more than human, their actions are also beyond human morality. The second subset is the single or small-scale homicidal maniac. This type has a wider range of visual appearance, from the maudlin to the traditional black. These villains take to heart a wound and thus seek recompense for some offense. Yet in both cases these villains must show themselves evil or capable of evil. They must become the foil of their paired hero.

He sees the sandpaper. The sound is awful, not like wood at all. The skin turns pink and then red and then bleeds. His arms, his face, his legs, back and chest; sweat and blood dripping on the floor.

Husband and wife sit quietly in the SUV as it cuts through the small snowdrifts in the midnight blue of early evening. Minutes pass before breath becomes invisible again in the growing heat of the vehicle. Henry turns on the radio, the news. There is a war somewhere getting worse, threatening to engulf the world, people are dying.

"He still needs that?" she asks.

"Yes," Henry answers.

Diana looks out the window and wipes the condensation with her hand. "Is it going to be a bad winter?"

"The summer was warm. The lake hasn't frozen yet."

"It will snow, then?"

"Yes," Henry answers.

"I like the winter, I missed it. The early winter anyway. Now is nice, before Christmas with the lights on the houses. It's almost peaceful. But not after the holidays. After New Year's it gets long and hard. They say many elderly and sick people die after the holidays. Nothing to look forward to, I suppose. It's only the cold. You look forward to the spring, to something that will change, the green grass, the warm air on your skin. You don't have to clench all the time. And it might be worth it, the wait, the anticipation, like Christmas. But what if the payoff, what if achieving your goal is a bitter disappointment? And it's not colossal or life changing. It's like you knew the end, you knew the prize wasn't that great, but you ignored those feelings and now you're forced to accept it and move on."

"Are you explaining something? Are you trying to tell me something? Are you telling me why you left?"

"No, it's not that. If I told you that, I'd have to tell why I came back."

The sky grows darker, the small streaks of the sun fall from the horizon. Arthur comes into view.

"He looks… bigger." Diana stares intently.

"Children grow quickly."

"Do you think he'll be happy to see me?"

"I'm not sure."

"But, do you think?"

"He might be."

Diana's breath fogs the window. Henry takes the SUV to the curb. Arthur pauses when sees his mother and waits, his head slightly tilted to the left. A wind whistles by, lifting the snow, swirling it about the boy. He remains in the midst of the small maelstrom, the center of it. Diana opens the door, the cold rushes in and Henry shivers.

"Hello, love." Diana's words are lost in the wind.

Arthur does not respond, but looks up at his mother.

"Climb aboard and we'll go home."

Arthur remains motionless, breathing through his scarf.

"C'mon now, love. Let's go home."

Arthur slowly, as if pushed, moves to the SUV. He sits in the front next to his father, forcing Diana to the back. The vehicle pulls away from the school as faces watch, pushed against the windows. The wind howls.

The vehicle glides through the snow, wrapped in a separate world. Speeches without voice, questions and revelations fill the cabin and filter through frosted windows.

"It's so dark," Diana whispers.

"It's the solstice today," Arthur answers. "The longest night of the year. Tomorrow it will start getting lighter. Tomorrow will change again."

"Will it?"

"Time moves forward," Arthur explains.

"How are you, love?"

"I'm fine, Mom. How have you been?"

"I missed you."

"Did you?"

"Yes."

"It snowed another half foot today."

"That's nice."

"Yes, it is."

The conversation continues, back and forth, until they reach home. Arthur disappears into the basement. Henry stands next to Diana in the kitchen. The house is dark, a deep gloom fills the rooms and hangs in the air.

"Do you have a bag? A suitcase?" Henry asks his wife.

"No. You should turn on some lights."

"I know," Henry replies.

She walks through the house and Henry follows.

"You put up the Christmas tree."

"Yes."

"And you decorated."

"Arthur said it was time."

"Yes, he would notice."

"Perhaps you should try talking to him again."

"Yes."

Diana leaves him and descends to the basement. Henry sighs and begins supper.

Episode 11: Secrets and Stories

He sees the tools, the ones that have been used and the ones that will be used. He must know that this is going to take some time, a long time. The hammer, the bat, the screwdriver, the sandpaper, the saw, the golf club, the everyday things that now seem terrible.

The attraction to the heroic ideal is the real center of the superhero. The reader is able to live out a fantasy of justice and power, wrapped in color and sound. The images draw the reader in and the notion that there is greatness in the world makes the hero remarkable. That somewhere out there, there are beings of wondrous powers and they fight equally deadly adversaries for noble reasons. It's the fantasy that touches us. We know most of what happens can never be true, but somewhere, down deep in all of us, is the hope that one day there will be an actual superhero.

It's time to start again. He watches. Draw out the decision, make him want one item over another. It's the potato peeler and he winces.

She's in bed, on her side. Henry is startled at first, having grown used to the emptiness of the room and now she's there.

"Are you all right with this?" she asks.

"Yes… no. It's a bit strange is all. You're back. I assumed you would…"

"Oh, the sleeping arrangements. I didn't know what else to do, where else to go. I missed this."

"Is that the reason?" Henry asks as he stands in the light of the adjacent bathroom, his shadow thrown on the wall. Diana lies still in the bed, the covers pulled up to her neck.

"Are you still looking for a reason?" she asks.

"Yes," he answers as he shuts off the bathroom light.

"Come here." She reaches for him.

Henry hesitates, his clothes suddenly tight about his skin. He strips and the clothes crumble to the floor. The snow reflects the streetlights and the room is a metallic blue. Henry sits on the edge of the bed with his back to Diana.

"Please, Henry. I'm very tired. It feels like I haven't slept for days."

"Can you tell me anything?"

Diana's head falls for a moment. Henry's eyes adjust to the light.

"I'll tell you where I was."

"That'll do."

Diana closes her eyes and takes a deep breath. "You know my parents weren't very religious. They were atheists." She pauses and thinks. "Ironically I wound up in a religious revival ministry."

Henry does not react.

"I know it sounds… like a story, but it's what happened." She pauses again and looks at Henry. He remains motionless. "I think what really drew me in was the pastor. He was such a strange looking man. He had this white skin, almost like a ghost, pale, but not reflective, sort of a dull white that absorbed the light." Diana shifts and the room grows warm.

"And jet black hair, shiny. He appeared sad to look at, his eyes turned down at the corners. They were gray and set deep in their sockets. His mouth was pink, almost red. He always wore a black suit with a white shirt, very stiff. His skin was warm all the time. He seemed to give off steam in cold weather. I was attracted... well not attracted, intrigued, I guess."

Henry sits quietly, listening.

"His voice was odd. High and low, depending on the word or sound, sort of an out of tune singsong quality. It took you off-guard, made you think the pastor was unreal."

"What was his name?"

"What?"

"His name."

"Oh." Diana pauses and clears her throat. "It's cold."

Henry turns his head slightly.

"Sekowsky, Michael Sekowsky was his name."

Henry nods.

"The Pastor, he liked to be called that, he would give these wonderful speeches."

"I think they're called sermons."

"Yes, well, these sermons were fantastic... no that's the wrong word. His words just washed over you. The actual words didn't mean anything. It was the delivery that took my imagination. Enthralling is a better description."

"Out of tune singsong?"

"Yes, the cadence and rhythm. The ideas were secondary. It was the performance. I felt I could do it. I could finally throw myself in utterly and not look back. I could follow him around the country, dispensing his message, passing out brochures. And I could listen to him speak and feel... protected... involved... like there was nothing else in the world."

"But you left."

"I left." She moves closer to him.

"Why?"

"I listened to the words one day. He was speaking to an audience, out west somewhere, a hot state, stale air, no breeze. And I heard the words. He said 'God wants me to tell you that doom is imminent. I believe this is why God has told me to warn every American and all the godless, subversive peoples of the world, all those who say they are Godly, but are not, that He is going to destroy you for your hypocrisy.'"

"This… Sekowsky said that?"

"Yes. He told the audience: 'On the day of judgment we'll account for our life.' God sent him with the message of his divine wrath."

"Whose wrath?"

"God's wrath. Pastor said: 'The end is coming. Giant locusts will rise out of a bottomless pit. Four of God's angels will slay one-third of all humankind.' He said we are very close to that moment."

"Did he give you any advice on how to avoid being part of the one-third?"

"He said I could become one of his prayer-warriors."

"And you liked that?"

Diana moves closer to him, almost touching. "There's something comforting in redemption. You have a chance to make good. I liked the idea of all or nothing for a while. Everything else is so… gray. With Pastor it was black or white. There was no middle ground, only good and evil, Satan or God. It was easy."

"But?"

"It was too easy. There's always a third choice or fourth or fifth, possibilities. Even in that atmosphere, I knew there was something else. I began to think about it, despite myself. Pastor continued to talk about the end of the world. He talked of the rapture. I think the idea of being chosen when others weren't appealed to him. But the idea struck me. I began to think the rapture had already occurred. I thought years ago, thousands of years ago it happened and God forgot about the rest of us, even forgot to destroy us. We're all the products of what was left behind: sinners who created another world from the ruins of a greater one. All this belief and religion and heaven and hell, it's nothing but a dream of a people who were not chosen."

"And that's when you left?"

"Soon after. I realized I couldn't listen to him anymore. I couldn't be humble in the face of his God. It didn't make sense anymore."

"And you came back?"

"Yes."

They sit for a time in the gloom. The wind is blowing beyond the walls of the house.

"And what of you, Hank? What happened to you?"

Henry slumps slightly then sits straight again. "I was lonely, of course."

"Have you seen the doctor lately?"

"No, no time. Arthur takes a lot of... you've seen the basement."

"Yes."

"I went out last week. Some guys from school took me to a place."

"That's nice."

"It was a strip club. They said I needed it."

Diana touches his back. "But the doctor and your pills?"

"I'm fine... that's fine. I went out with Allen and Jordan. They said it would be good for me."

"Oh... and what happened. You wanted me to ask, didn't you?"

"It was fine. The place was dark inside, long shadows with neon lights. The tables shook, pounding music, like thunder, like a storm."

"That's..."

He turns to look at her. Her skin is glowing in the dark room. He follows the light to the blanket, engulfed in black.

Just her skin is there, her arm, her face, no eyes, no hair, just the shell, the iridescent shell in a black ocean.

"What is it, Henry?"

"Nothing. There's nothing."

"What happened with Allen and Jordan?"

"They wanted me to have a lap dance. Do you know what that is?"

"Yes."

"In college we would go to strip clubs and get lap dances."

"Hmm."

He wonders what he looks like to Diana. If he seems like a ghost, his face floating before her. There and not there.

"I didn't want to get one. It seemed odd, out of place really. A strange woman writhing about on top of me. I thought I seemed too old for it."

"That's a strange thing to think."

"I suppose."

"You didn't feel guilty about demeaning a woman, setting back equal rights, turning back the clock to when women were objects?"

He can see her smile, imagined, beautiful beguiling smile. "You can't demean someone bent on demeaning themselves."

"Yes."

"I was drinking. That's what depressed and lonely people do."

"Are you depressed?"

An awkward silence, half a second long.

"My wife had left me."

"You didn't know I was coming back?"

"Yes… no. You were still gone."

"Hmm."

"It happened Allen told a stripper to take me in the back room and not to take no for an answer."

"You were forced?"

"Yes." Henry swings his legs on the bed and leans against the headboard next to her. "She sat me down in the back room. She was talking to me. Telling me it was all paid for, that she was paid for and all I had to do was enjoy myself. She was going to make me happy. She called me 'baby'. She smelled different, like something I'd never smelled before. There was a perfume about her skin and hair. Her skin was smooth, a deep and endless black."

"She was black? Playing out some long held fantasy?"

"She was different, different from each other one. But she kept talking, telling me she had a great body, not beautiful or intoxicating, but great. She repeated it over and over. I asked her to stop speaking and to stop moving and I held her... held her close to me for my allotted time."

"What happened?"

"Nothing. We sat there. I thought I needed something. It was like seeing myself from outside. She told me my time was up and I left her."

"Did you say anything else?"

"I didn't think I was supposed to." Henry shifts and the wind howls beyond the house.

"Why not?"

"I'm not sure."

"I would think it would be easy to make something up," Diana whispers.

Henry is quiet. The house shakes gently.

"She's naked, right?" Diana asks. "She's vulnerable, the most vulnerable a person can be. You could have told her anything and she would've been accepting. She wouldn't insult you or upset you. She would listen and respond honestly. I would think it's the easiest time to talk to someone when they're naked. You could release yourself with her, unburden your soul. Touch her and talk. Find a moment of connection. False or genuine, it wouldn't matter. You might have been happy."

"Why did you come back?"

"It was time."

"Why did you leave?"

"Ask me tomorrow."

She moves closer, taking the sheets and wrapping them around Henry, cocooning them against the cold

"Do you want me to stay here?" Henry asks.

"Yes."

He slouches in the bed, his head next to hers, the smell of her skin, the smell of her hair about him. The wind bellows and the house shakes.

Episode 12: The Coldness of the World

I am the wind, the snow and the unrelenting cold. I am part of the landscape, part of the greater whole. My actions cannot be understood. My actions cannot be analyzed. I am compelled, like the heroes of old. I am not of this time or this reality.

There's a party in the dead of winter. A Christmas party, perhaps. Christ and all. But they mock the season of family and cheer. Those inside follow the ancient traditions. The feast of Saturis lives again with all its debauchery and deviant forms of worship. But that doesn't matter. Notions of celebrations, ancient forms of felicity are of no concern. There is only good and evil in the world, in the night of cold and snow.

There he is, the heat escaping with him. He travels with others, his acolytes. Have to fight through the lieutenants, but that's no matter, no matter at all. They walk between the houses, the maze of the suburb, the labyrinth of large homes and patios. Some stumble and fall and laugh. Drunk or high. Their laughter does not echo, caught in the wind. They don't think of their victims, they don't consider the innocent of the world. It's already too late. One falls in a cloud of white while the others move on, leaving him giggling in the deep snow.

The boy's face changes as a shadow appears above him. He asks for help. He swears when none is offered. The attack is swift and merciless. The boy is left well enough to run away, to tell his leader that the night has come for vengeance, has come on behalf of all the victims who can no longer sleep, for all the nameless and the faceless that need protection. A hero has come.

"That's why they're all moving?"

"Yes, it's in the air. They can sense it. People can do that, you know? I saw it on TV. A man swore he could see God and angels."

"Really?"

"Yes. It was neat. He was excited about it. He said he could talk to God."

"Is that so? Do you like syrup?"

Henry enters the kitchen, groggy, half-awake, the world a blur. The room smells good, comforting, home-like. It's not the morning for waffles, however. Today is eggs, two, and two sausage patties. Waffles are for Sunday.

"Morning, sleepy-head," Diana says as she kisses her husband on the cheek.

"Huh…"

"Mom, don't you want to hear about the man?"

"Oh yes, love. Arthur was telling me about this man who says…"

"What time is it?" Henry asks, blurting out the words.

"What dear? It's early, six-thirty."

"Six?" Henry's world hardens, edges appear.

"Yes. I'm making breakfast. Would you like a waffle?" Diana dances a bit, holding a waffle before her husband.

"Arthur… you're up."

"Yes, Dad. I was watching the storm. I watched the news to see what happened."

"Oh."

"Yes, I heard the television and I got up to see if it was you." Diana pats Arthur's head as she turns to Henry. "You didn't have to sleep in the spare bedroom."

"I just..."

"It's fine. I understand. So I found him watching the news. His school is closed. Yours isn't. Have to educate the youth, I'm afraid. Fight the flood of ignorance and all that."

"Arthur, you're eating...waffles."

"It's okay, Dad. She didn't know the routine. It'll be okay."

"Our son is very considerate with the new chef." She kisses Arthur on the head and sits next to him.

"Yeah... okay... well... so," Henry stammers.

"There's coffee." She smiles at her husband. "Now tell me, my love, tell me about the man who talked to God."

Henry looks for a moment: peace, contentment, but already anticipating the feelings' eventual demise. He turns and shuffles to the shower, a cup of coffee in his hand.

In the car Henry listens to the morning news read by an old man and his young female partner. The old man talks about the weather and the roads and how they're both very dangerous today. Not the road itself, but what has happened to the road, the condition of the road. The original idea of the road remains sound, remains as it was designed to be, just dangerous now, different from what it was. The woman tells Henry to be careful of the roads because they've changed. The man reads the list of school closings, too dangerous for the children to risk school, too perilous to venture outside. Henry is careful. He avoids the plows and the salt trucks, weaving in and out. The man's voice is comforting, like he really cares about Henry and really wants him to be safe. Henry smiles.

Henry's school is cold. The blood is slow to warm the extremities; toes and fingers are numb, except for the subtle sensation of the cold creeping in. Several children murmur near their lockers, taking layer after layer off.

Henry enters his room and the heater whines. He touches it, cold, the fan hums, but there is no heat. The windows are frosted over, a sheet of ice clings to the glass. Henry removes his coat and sits behind his desk. Papers are organized in piles, little Johnny Jones's work corrected. Except for the cold everything is as it should be. He turns on the computer and a picture of Arthur and his mother comes into focus. It was his favorite when she was gone. It reminded him of better days, a sliver of time frozen with smiles and sun at the park, before the boy developed quirks and needs, before Diana left and came back. Henry smiles.

He checks the inter-office email. There's a message from O'Brien, asking to see him today. It was posted an hour ago. Noise in the hall draws Henry's attention and he looks up quickly and then back to the computer. An image circles in his head: the doorway, the boy. He looks up again.

Nothing. But he was there, Henry is sure. The villain himself. Perhaps he knows, perhaps he saw. Henry leans back waiting. Students enter quietly, placing their books on their desks, mumbling about the snow. Henry has an urge to go into the hall, see if he's still there, around the corner. But he simply reminds the students present that there are worse things in the world than a cold school.

"That cocksucker." Jordan spits bits of donut as he speaks. "A fucking superintendent's hearing about my competence. Fuck her."

Henry pours coffee, the residual steam is thicker than yesterday.

"Hey, Hank," Allen greets him.

"Fuck this place," Jordan whispers through clenched teeth.

"He's in a mood," Henry says as he stirs his coffee.

Allen remains silent.

"Fuck this place."

The door opens as Jordan speaks. Two female teachers pause. They look at Jordan and shake their heads. They whisper quickly and leave.

"Fuck them too."

"Take it easy, Barry," Allen says.

"Fuck." Jordan sits with a sigh.

Henry takes his place at the opposite end of the table. There is silence for a moment, only the sound of the struggling heater fills the space between the three teachers. "So what's the story?" Henry asks.

"She's fucking me. Tomorrow I have to go to a hearing about my grades and conduct."

"Conduct?" Henry stops mid-sip.

"It's bullshit, Hank."

Henry looks at Allen. "They're saying Barry hit a kid," Allen announces gravely.

"What?"

"It's ..." Jordan looks out the window at the blowing snow. Great clouds are taken from the roof and thrown to the sky, scattered and lost.

Allen lowers his voice and leans closer to Henry, serious, the usual smile runs straight and the normally bright eyes grow narrow. "He's supposed to go home. They've called in a sub for him. They say he's unfit to be with children. You know how it is with this sort of thing, guilty and proven guilty. I'm going with him. I don't think... he doesn't seem well enough to drive himself. O'Brien is calling people in to give statements. It's a witch-hunt now. It's got a life of its own now. This is going to be bad."

"Is there anything I can do?" Henry looks at Jordan, who stares into the snow and the wind and the cold. His face seems white, reflecting the light, no life of its own.

"No. Nothing. You'll probably be called," Allen says.

"I got an email."

"Be careful."

"I guess I'll have to be." Henry pauses for moment and looks at his coffee, the cream separating slightly. "Did he…"

Allen adjusts his eyeglasses and wipes them with a napkin. "He needs to get out of here. He needs some space."

"Is he going to be fired?"

"Maybe. I mean the kid said that Barry punched or slapped him. He's got a bruise. He's a trouble-maker, parents didn't care about him until this."

"When did it happen?"

"Allegedly happen, remember that, Hank. Yesterday afternoon, after school."

"Yesterday seems a world away now," Jordan announces to the room.

"We should get going."

Henry stands with Allen. "Are your classes covered?" Henry asks.

"Yes. I already talked to O'Brien. I'm all set." Allen looks at Jordan.

"Seems the world is crumbling and all that's left isn't worth a damn. It's enough to make you want to give up," Jordan says as he walks in front of Allen. Allen whispers something in his ear and puts his arm around his colleague. They leave quietly, close together. Henry walks behind them to the building exit. He watches as they disappear into the snow.

Episode 13: Truth and Justice

O'Brien is sitting behind her desk when Henry enters her office. She again seems intent on the papers before her. The blinds are drawn and the overhead light is a pale yellow.

"O'Brien." Henry says her name cautiously.

"Hello, Hank. Sit down. I just have to finish this."

"If it's a bad time, I can come back later."

"No. Have to get this done. It's been a rough week, with the hazing incident and the car accident and-"

"What accident?"

"Parent called this morning. She said her son was in an accident last night. Damn snow. I guess it was pretty bad by her account. Broken bones and such."

"Who was it?"

"Nigma, Eric Nigma. Do you know him?"

"No. I don't think so."

"Tough kid, had him in my office a couple of times, but still, you don't like to see that happen to anyone." O'Brien moves quickly, signing her name, shuffling, glancing at her computer.

Henry looks about the office and sits quietly with his hands folded. A picture of Nigma's face, blood splattered, wheezing, crying floats before his mind's eye.

"Who was that boy that was in here yesterday?"

"What's that?" O'Brien sips her coffee and signs something, her eyes moving quickly.

"That boy, yesterday he was in your office."

O'Brien reads something from her computer and writes a note. "I'm sorry. I don't remember."

"He was in here yesterday. A boy, I don't know his name. I think he's a troublemaker. I thought you were talking to him about the hazing incident. Dinah told me."

"I'm sorry. That doesn't ring a bell."

"Yesterday." Henry's hands press on the principal's desk. "You talked to him before I spoke to you yesterday."

"I'm not sure. Just let me finish this." Her hands move above the papers, not touching any, but moving, always moving.

"Dinah saw him. She told me."

"What's that Hank? Who are you talking about?" She takes another sip from her mug.

"A student, a boy..." Henry trails off suddenly. They've gotten to her. Something in her movements, a code revealing a mystery, help me, save me. "How's your boy?" Henry asks.

O'Brien stops abruptly, eyes focused on her desk, minor tremors of involuntary movement in her hands. "What?"

"Your boy, your son, how is he?"

"He's fine... fine. So much going on right now. I feel like I never see him."

"Yes." Henry sits back and takes it all in, thinking it through.

"Now, we should talk about Jordan." O'Brien looks at Henry for the first time.

"Yes."

"I'm sure you've heard what's happened?"

Afraid of them, afraid of their threats. War is brutal. War has casualties. But you cannot weaken, cannot give in. "No, not really."

"You may know that Jordan was under review for his lack of appropriate grades on the state assessment."

Ruled by fear. "Yes, I heard something about that."

"That's not why you're here. There's been something else. A..."

"Incident?"

"Look, I know you're his friend, but I have a situation here." She seems serious.

"I understand, but I don't know anything about this incident."

O'Brien stares at Henry. "He's been accused of assaulting a student. I cannot divulge the name of the child, but there is strong evidence of abuse."

Save you anyway, despite your weakness. "Abuse?"

"Maybe that's too harsh. The student claims that Jordan hit him in the hallway after school. There are witnesses who corroborate the story."

"That's hard to believe."

"Is it? There has to be an investigation." O'Brien pauses and composes herself and represses the slight breaks in her professional demeanor. "Have you ever heard of Jordan, in any way, abuse or physically manhandle a student?"

Henry assesses the situation before answering. She's trying to keep the fear from gaining control, O'Brien couldn't bear it, no parent could.

"Should I have a union rep with me?" Henry asks.

"No, no. This is an informal interview," O'Brien responds.

"Can you tell me who Jordan allegedly assaulted?"

O'Brien shifts slowly in her chair, her head falls and she places her pen on the desk gently, motherly, careful not to disturb any of the papers. "I can't tell you that. He's still under investigation. In the end it doesn't matter who the child is."

"I see."

"So, Hank, have you ever heard of Barry being abusive to any of the students?"

"No."

"What about anyone else? His wife? Have you ever heard anything about the reason why he got divorced?"

"Does that matter?"

"Pattern of behavior."

"Pattern?"

"Maybe he's been abusive before." O'Brien does not look at Henry. She gazes at the pen amongst the clutter of her desk.

"If he did, which I think is unlikely, it shouldn't have any relevance on this current set of circumstances."

O'Brien looks up, her face is serene and quiet. She seems gray, her light blue eyes ghostlike, there and not there. "Our past is always relevant, Hank. It's the only thing that is in the end. What we did or what we were before is important. For us as adults, the past, our past is us. It's different for the younger ones, our children, for them it's the future, but for us it's our past. That's the definition of who we are."

"O'Brien?"

"Sorry." She leans back in the shadows. "I'm a bit out of sorts. There's a great deal going on right now, so much to think about. But no need no lay that on you."

"No, I mean, it's okay. We could... talk."

"You're right. Neither the time nor the place. Stay on task. Remember the conference last year? Know your present reality." She chuckles. "Because what came before doesn't matter." She smiles slightly.

"O'Brien, are you all right?"

"I'm fine. So, you say no history, nothing violent in his past. There's nothing in his file. Just this one incident and the man is ruined."

"Ruined?"

"Fired. Can't have the bad press. He'll be let go. There's no saving him."

"Isn't there anything?"

"Thanks for listening, Hank. I guess that's all."

The whirl of papers begins again and O'Brien is lost in her world of reports and test scores.

Henry watches for a moment and then leaves.

Episode 14: Geniuses and Madmen

It's not snowing, but the wind blows without pause. Great clouds of snow are formed and then vanish among the gray sky and the gray buildings as Henry trudges to his car. The day was a waste. His classes would not let go of the ever-evolving story of Mr. Jordan and how he slapped a kid, fought a kid, punched a kid, touched a kid. Henry refused to acknowledge the growing narrative and gave a quiz long enough to fill each period. He doesn't blame his students, mixture of fear and excitement and curiosity, but he had had enough and wanted quiet. Some asked their Math teacher if he knew the truth. Henry replied that he did not and told them to be quiet.

In the parking lot, he fumbles with his keys as the wind gusts.

"Henry."

The wind calls to him. Too emotional, too involved.

"Hank."

Henry turns to find Mr. Lance behind him, windows down, motor running.

"Oh, hey Ollie."

"Do you have a minute, Henry?"

"Sure." Henry walks over to his colleague.

"We can't talk here, have to yell everything." The wind blows with indifferent fury.

"Hmm."

"Get in," Mr. Lance says as he looks about.

"What?"

"We should go somewhere warm, so we can talk. I have something to tell you."

"Now? Couldn't this wait?"

"Please, Henry. This is important to me."

"Well, I mean Diana is home with Arthur, but..."

"There, you see." Mr. Lance pushes open the passenger side door. Henry gets into the car after a moment's hesitation.

The radio is on, a soft voice, religious fervor, a believer, true and blind faith. Henry looks out the window. "Where are we going?" he asks.

"The bar down the street. It's quiet and we can talk."

Henry has an urge to reply, a witty remark or a joke, but he doesn't and continues to look out the window. Lance drives quickly, taking turns without really slowing down. He pulls into the parking lot and the car lurches to a stop.

The bar is dark, a profound bleakness welcomes patrons as they step in from the cold. A lone figure sits at the opposite end of the establishment. The form, man or woman, does not look up or move in the slightest manner when the two men enter. Mr. Lance scans the interior, eyes growing accustomed to the soft yellow light.

"Over there, we'll go over there." Mr. Lance's cadence is quick. He touches Henry's shoulder.

They sit at a table along the wall between two windows. The gray of the outside world filters in on either side. Henry notices the bartender has appeared, an older woman, big hair, owner probably, happy in the dim light, her place now, long days of work, long hours, long life and the bar is doing fine, everything is fine, even that doctor's appointment about her grandson will be fine. She stands behind the bar looking at them.

"I think we should order something," Henry whispers. His words do not disturb the air currents or the atmosphere, not even a ripple.

"Right, right." Mr. Lance hustles to the bar, dust trailing behind him and returns to the table. "I got you a beer. You drink beer, right?"

"That's fine." Henry resists using his power on Mr. Lance. "What are you having?" he asks.

"Water, just water."

"You don't drink beer? I didn't know that. I thought all teachers drank. Especially on days like this."

"I do drink. I mean I did drink, but just not now." Lance pauses and looks at Henry, his head cocked to one side. "What happened today?"

"Didn't you hear about Jordan?"

"Oh that. I heard about that. I thought you were talking about…"

"What?"

"Nothing."

Henry almost reaches out to Lance, across the table with his power, but swigs his beer instead. It's been a while since he had a drink, since Diana left. She's back though. "That tastes good."

"Hmm." Mr. Lance stares at his hands, folded before him, gathering himself. Henry drinks again.

"Hank," Lance begins in a quiet voice, "I've been working on something lately. Well, not lately, a while now… a long while it seems."

Henry nods. "I know. You were out."

"Yes. It needed time. I needed time to figure it out."

Henry nods and sips his beer.

"And it's come to this." Mr. Lance pauses and touches his glass of water. "I'm convinced the world is coming to an end."

Henry takes the bottle from his lips. "What?"

"Hear me out. I've told no one. You're the first. Even I want to hear what it sounds like out loud. You're like me, well, I think you're like me. I know math. I trust math. It's the only thing that's never let me down, never lied to me."

"Yes," Henry responds.

"I've been doing calculations since I was child. I was very good... I am very good at calculations. I graduated high school early, college too. It's the patterns, you see? I can see them, the way things fit together. And I've calculated the world is coming to an end."

"Ollie, this is a bit-"

"Listen closely," Mr. Lance whispers, imperative that his secret becomes known. "This is the key. There is no set pattern. I was wrong to look for it or look for it in the understood terms of patterns. It's the randomness of things. Put that together and you've got your answer."

"Ollie, I-"

"Hank, please follow along. The random numbers of the world, that's the bulk of it, the middle. All I needed was the beginning and the end. The last two integers of the equation."

Henry concentrates: focus, joy, perfection, a drive never felt before. "This is-"

"Yes, it is. You see, no one would understand but you. The numbers added, subtracted, divided, multiplied, the giant puzzle of the world, and it's always been there. Take the length of a 1975 Chevrolet Corvette, multiply by the age of Christ when he gave the sermon on the mount, add the ages of Moses and Buddha when they died, divide by the date of the Russian Revolution and subtract the date of the first known Atomic test, divide by the average bust size of every playmate between 1980 and 1997, add the number of times the word death is used in Hamlet, and hundreds of other random variables, add, subtract, multiply, divide and so on. You get the same number again and again. All I needed was the starting point, something marked on my personal conscious. Different and the same, you see? We each have that different starting point, but the end, the final answer is always the same. I just needed my starting point."

"Ollie, you can't be serious. This is-"

"No, no, think it through. The great randomness of the world and yet not random at all. A system to give us our answer. It's just finding that starting point."

"Starting point?"

"Yes, yes, that's what was eluding me. I tried my birthday, social security number, pin numbers-"

"Why not zero?"

"Hank, you know nothing starts with zero. There is always at least some value, positive or negative, something is always the starting factor." Mr. Lance pauses, waiting for acknowledgement. Henry fingers his empty beer bottle. "So as I was saying, I looked everywhere for my starting point, my number. Anniversaries, wife's birthday-"

"Where is your wife?"

Mr. Lance's shoulders slump. His face recedes into the shadows. "There must be sacrifices for all great knowledge, I suppose. Something must be given up for the answer."

"What happened?"

"To tell the truth, Hank, I'm not sure what became of her. One day I realized she wasn't there anymore. I had been wrapped in this formula for so long, months I guess. I had been cruel, I suppose. I didn't pay any attention and she left. It was what had to happen. In the end she wasn't that important."

"Not important?" Henry knocks over the bottle, startled by his own quickness to anger. He leans into Mr. Lance. "Jesus, you don't even know what happened to her. She could be dead. She could be hurt."

"I don't think so. I think I would have known that."

"You're crazy. I mean, you really have gone off the deep end."

"Don't call me that. Don't call me that." Mr. Lance gazes at his hands again.

"What else are you then? Your wife is gone and you didn't even notice?"

"What did you do when your wife left?" Lance asks.

The anger dissipates as quickly as it came, like snow caught in a gust. "I…"

"My wife had her own path. We were together and then we weren't. I'm sure she's fine, probably better without me. That was the end of us and I had more important things to think about. It's like the Jordan business. It doesn't really matter. These small things are inconsequential. Only the big picture matters. Fundamental forces at work, the grand scheme, whatever you choose to call it. All other things are meaningless. All other things are numbers in the equation."

"People are not numbers," Henry whispers.

"Yes and no. Social security numbers, pin numbers, security codes, bar codes, all numbers to be used. It's all the numbers of the world, the wonderful randomness of numbers. All you need is-"

"The starting point."

"Yes." Mr. Lance sips his water. "Would you like another beer?"

"No. I think… I think I should get home."

"Diana is back?"

"Yes."

"She's come back for a reason," Lance whispers.

"Ollie-"

"I don't want to upset you. I'll take you back. We can talk more another time. It was just good to get that out."

Henry rises silently. The bartender nods to them as they leave. The car ride back to the school parking lot is quiet. As Henry is about to exit the car into the snow globe world, he asks, "What was your starting point?"

Mr. Lance smiles. "My friend was shot. He was that principal who saved those kids a while back. It was the time I learned that he had been shot, the numbers on the digital clock."

Mr. Lance pulls away in a cloud of snow. Henry scrapes the ice from his windshield. The sound does not echo.

Epilogue to Episode 14

"Ridiculous. Out of his mind. And he works with children. Randomness of numbers. Insane, just insane. The starting point? What the hell does that mean? He's broken. Maybe he has a history. The stories about him. Totally gone. And he's not coming back. Math works. Math is clear. Not some jumble of signs and symbols. Formulas work. End of the world? He said that, actually said it out loud. End of the world. Stupid to even think of it. Can't be true. Things make sense in math. His equation isn't honest. Wrong word. Honesty isn't an option, not even a consideration. Math is above honesty and truth and sanity. The problem is too vague. It needs parameters, a shape, a definition. That's the whole basis of math. There is an exact solution and an exact formula for it. Cut and dry, black and white. Randomness of numbers. Crazy old man. Crazy, lonely old man."

Could be comic book numbers?

"It's silly, really."

Batman's height and weight?

"Stupid, random numbers and some formula to put them in. Stupid."

The issue Superman dies, but didn't really die?

"No point in considering it. Laugh at it. One big joke."

First appearance of Aquaman?

"Seventy-three, *More Fun Comics*, but it's a joke. Diana will laugh when I tell her."

The year the first *Justice League* came out?

"1961. But still, where would I find my starting point?"

No, it was in *The Brave and the Bold*, that's the first appearance of the Justice League.

"1960 then. But how would I know? How did Lance know?"

Maybe you just know.
"Maybe you're right, Carter. Maybe you just know."

Episode 15: Cityscapes and Vanishing Points

He finds Diana and Arthur in the basement. Arthur is busy among his citizens. Diana is watching him, sipping tea, an open book on her lap.

"Hey, Dad," Arthur says, not looking up.

"How goes the city?" Henry asks.

"Too early to tell."

Henry nods and looks at Diana. She smiles, beautiful, rapturous, lovely. "And how are you?" Henry sits next to her.

"Fine. We've had a full day. Went to lunch and took some pictures. New people. It's nice to have new people I was told." She smiles at Arthur. "I asked about having some music down here, a soundtrack for the city, but he said no, didn't you, love? Each person has their own soundtrack."

Arthur bustles about, moving this and that, life and death. Henry glances at his son and back at his wife and grins. Starting points and ending points.

"I should start dinner," Diana announces and rises and kisses Henry gently. "You've been drinking?" She looks surprised, then a slight look of concern comes across her face.

"Ollie Lance wanted to talk about something after school. We went to a bar."

"No need to explain." She kisses him again, pressing harder, and walks upstairs.

Arthur looks at his father. "She moved. I think she's in a better place now," he announces.

"What?" Henry looks at his son, glassy eyed.

"In the city. She moved closer to you. Do you like that? I thought you would like that. She's near you now."

"I'm in your city?"

"Yes. You live there, by the water. It's called Coast City. It's pretty. You can see the water and the park. You like it there."

"I'm happy?"

"No, not really. You have other things that worry you."

"What?"

Arthur frowns.

"I forgot. I don't get to know. But how about this one time? It's my life after all."

"You have secrets. You know things and that worries you."

"That makes sense."

Henry does not push the conversation, preoccupied with something else. Arthur continues to watch him for a moment longer and then goes back to the bustle of life. Henry sits in the corner, by the computer. The space heater hums and glows orange. Arthur casts a shadow over skyscrapers made of milk cartons, painted gray with small yellow windows. Shadows hide in a few of the windows, faceless lives living in the cardboard world.

They eat dinner together, talking lightly of the weather and the fact Christmas is only a few days away. Arthur tells the story of his city's need to decorate, different cultures celebrating different things. He has devised his own religion, practiced by a select few in the city, only nine percent by his estimation. They worship silently in their temple, focusing on a series of candles on an altar. There is incense and soft music. He explains that the senses are the primary method of knowing a greater power. Visions often come to the parishioners. There are no seats, only rugs on a clean floor. There are no windows and the inside of the temple is kept cold, sometimes they see their own breath. The sole purpose of worship is knowing the next world, understanding that this world it is not important. Henry and Diana listen intently. They smile at each other.

The remainder of the evening is spent watching television. Thirty seconds here and there, a flicker of light across their faces. At the exact and appropriate time Arthur goes to bed. Henry and Diana follow soon after.

Henry is removing his pants when Diana asks, "What did Lance want?" She slips beneath the covers.

Henry sits on the bed in his underwear. "Nothing really. Just to talk about something he's been working on."

"He was strange, but nice in an old-man sort of a way."

"Yeah." Henry tosses his clothes in the hamper and walks to the bathroom. It smells of Diana now, a day later, and the smell of her lotions fills him.

"I'll do laundry tomorrow," she calls out.

Henry returns to the bed. "Thanks."

She moves next to him and pushes herself against him. "Will you be here in the morning?"

"Yes," Henry whispers and turns out the light.

The wind has calmed. The snow reflects the now exposed moon and the world is a soft white. The mounds of snow seem as gentle undulations on the earth. The bedroom is quiet, except for the heater's hum, forcing warmth into the room. The curtains move with subtle waves, the circulation of the warmed air. The light of the room, reflected off the snow and moon makes the air seem silver and precious, giving the remaining colors that hue also, as if touched by something better and wonderful.

"What was he working on?" Diana asks.

"Lance?"

"Yes."

"It's stupid, you'll laugh."

"Now you must tell me."

"He told me he's figured out the end of the world, when it will happen."

"Really?"

"Yes. He is quite convinced he has it all worked out."

"Did he tell you the date?"

"No." Henry looks at her, white skin and dark hair, barely there in the silver darkness. "I didn't ask."

"Seems like an important thing to know."

"It was a joke."

"He was joking?"

"No... I mean yes. He was serious, but I took it as a joke."

"But it wasn't joke to him?"

"No. He was sure."

Diana closes her eyes, the deep and fathomless canyons of her eyes.

"It's ridiculous though. I mean, knowing the end of the world, equations and starting points..."

"What?"

"Starting points. He went on and on about starting points. You can't figure out the answer without the starting point."

"Makes sense, I guess, in a way."

"I suppose."

The night stretches out across the world. The snow is touched by a light wind, but remains for the most part, unmovable and inexorable.

Episode 16: The Hand of Fate

What's he thinking about? What could he possibly be thinking about?

The origin of a hero is crucial to the development of that hero's overall mission and worldview. Usually there's a tragedy. All the great ones have a tragic past. Murder of parents, destruction of a planet, an original failure to be reconciled. But the irony of the hero's origin story is that it is very similar to the origin story of the villain. They too have a tragedy to compensate for. The difference is strength of will. The hero carries on in a world that is chaotic and the villain gives into that chaos. The villain welcomes the advancing darkness while the hero strives against it. But the initial tragedy is there in both of them: death, loss, abandonment; the outsider trying to fit in. It's why the battles between the truly great heroes and the truly great villains are so epic. The same motivation, the same will to make up for a loss drives them both. It's poetic and beautiful. The sane world, the real world looks askance at this dance. The real world questions it and ridicules it, but could never understand it, never really understand it.

He's struggling. Maybe he's thinking about what will happen next. The bat, the golf club, the hammer. He's thinking it through. Even when the blade is pulled across his arm, he's thinking of what he'll do after.

"I guess they think it's safer if they just stay home."

"You don't mind, do you? I could call in."

"Mind? No. He's my son. Why would I mind?"

"No reason, I guess."

"Hmm."

"I should get going then. I have a stop to make before I go to school."

"Cheer up, Hank. It's Friday after all."

"I'm fine."

"Sure you are. You seem preoccupied."

"Something at school."

"That Lance thing?"

"No. Yes. I guess that's on my mind too."

"But there's something else?"

"You remember Barry Jordan?"

"Yes. He was at the Christmas party. Loud fellow."

"Yeah. He might get fired."

"Oh."

"So I'm going to meet him for coffee before school."

"That's why you're up so early? It's like you haven't slept at all."

"Yes."

"Don't worry about Arthur and me."

"Okay, I won't." Henry shuffles to the bathroom.

The man in the mirror looks tired. His hand moves out on instinct, touching the image. He washes, taking time to look into the red eyes and the growing dark circles beneath those orbs.

"I should be right home after school," he announces as he returns to the bedroom, dressed and presentable.

"And tonight you'll stay with me?" Diana asks.

"Yes, tonight I'll stay." He kisses her, warm in bed, and walks away.

The waitress smiles at him. He's been here before, a regular on certain Fridays, having breakfast with colleagues before the school day starts. The sun has come out and the restaurant is bright, almost blinding. The snow reflects the light, like white glass. The cold remains however, but the blinding white is all encompassing. It attacks the eye, penetrating into the mind in a great flash, resetting thoughts and dreams.

Allen and Jordan sit in a booth, waiting and sipping steaming coffee. Allen rises at Henry's approach and sits next to Jordan.

"Morning, Hank," Allen says with a smile.

"Hey guys." Henry sits and coffee is placed before him. "How's everything?"

"What do you mean?" Jordan asks as he stares at the window, peering right through the reflecting sun.

"Just… well everything from yesterday."

"Nothing new," Jordan whispers.

"Are you going in today?" Henry asks Allen.

"No. I called in sick. Most schools are closed anyhow. Too cold."

"Oh."

Jordan continues to look out the window, interested in every angle and aspect of the world. "To think, it's come to this," he says.

"What's that?" Allen's voice is soft, gentle and friendly.

Jordan sips his coffee. "Everything I've done, everything that's been done to me, all the events and decisions I've made and I'm here, in this place, drinking coffee." He takes another sip. Allen watches him as does Henry. "And it's so early in the morning and so bright. You see the sun stepping over the horizon, reds and yellows and dark blues and it's beautiful. I know it's beautiful and magnificent and glorious and hundreds of other words. But for a long time I couldn't see it. And to be perfectly honest I still can't really see it, can't appreciate it. I don't know it beyond the fact that it's going to happen. And the world will be white, a great, vast, endless white." He pauses and smiles at his coffee. "The whiteness of the whale." He looks at Allen, then at Henry. "White is the absence of all color. Did you know that? Like the white whale. I used to read, before I had to teach reading. I read the great books because I loved them. I loved *Moby Dick*. The white whale and the white world. 'Nothing in you now but the cadence of the sea' or something like that. I haven't thought about that in a long time, like the sunrise. I didn't think about it because I had to think about my job or my wife or test scores or the car or all the other shit that made up my life."

Henry clears his throat, looks at Allen, and sips his coffee.

"Those things were important and the sunrise wasn't, neither was *Moby Dick*, not really. But now I'm here and suddenly all that matters is watching the sunrise and the world will flash white. And I'll sit here and take it in and I'll think about it and think what will happen after. I'm not sure that this is important, but I thought it and I thought I should say it. Can I get out of the booth, Hal? I have to use the bathroom."

Allen pauses and then moves. Jordan smiles and walks slowly to the lavatory. Henry sits wide-eyed, mouth slightly open, waiting for Allen to speak. He doesn't, but stirs his coffee in the growing light of morning.

"Jesus," whispers Henry.

"What?"

"That... that... what he said. I mean, what was that?"

"Him, I suppose, or what he is now."

Henry tenses slightly, his power waking. "Allen, seriously, is he okay?"

"I don't know. I guess. Who's to say?"

"But that, that outburst? I mean, I've never seen him like that. Have you?"

"From time to time. During his divorce or when change happens to him. He thinks about it, contemplates the events that led to the change. He looks for meaning in the afterward. It's who he is."

Henry sits back and touches his spoon, the metal is cold.

"You should probably order, Hank. It's getting late."

"What about you?"

"I guess we're staying here for a while. No need to rush."

"You're staying with him?"

"He's going to talk some more and I'll listen."

"That's it?"

"What else is there?"

Henry looks out the window and at the grand sky beyond, erupting now in fire and light. "Tell him I had to go."

"I will," Allen responds with a smile.

Henry walks into the open world and gets into his car. Great snowdrifts line the streets to school. There have been accidents recently, sudden crashes of mortality on the way to the mall or dinner. Henry drives carefully, aware of other motorists. He takes his time, wanting to live, to see what will happen. As he pulls into the parking lot, the school remains a dark shadow against the building sky.

Episode 17: Destiny is in the Details

The day proceeds without incident. Students pass before him, questions and answers, futures and pasts. He teaches numbers and symbols, problems and solutions, mundane and monumental. Worksheets, quizzes, tests, papers upon papers collected and dispersed, names and faces, soon children of children. The years stretch from this day to the last day and he'll be remembered here and there, by one student or another. 'Remember that Math teacher?' An anecdote, laughing years from now, in their memory, not distinct, not exact, faded by shadow, but there in the recesses of their brains: that Math teacher 'What was his name?' Some won't recall and some will, 'His name was short. Dent or something like that.'

Henry sits at his desk, the final bell echoing in the background, the subtle flutter of life carried out of the room. He sits deflated, slumped in his chair staring at his desk, coffee cup, protractor, compass, calculator, grade book with names and grades, more numbers, rewards for being right and punishments for being wrong. Beneath is a calendar again marked with names, a birthday here and there. To the corner of the desk is a picture of Arthur, older, posed for Christmas, his small hands folded under his chin. It's cold in the room and he

91

shivers. The heater struggles continually to push back the icy hands. Henry knows the winter will linger long into March, touching days in April with a threatening chill.

The sounds from the hall die away. Henry closes his eyes and thinks of Friday and the weekend and Diana. He looks up and Lance is standing in his room. The old man's tie is tight against his collar and yet his clothes hang loosely, bought when he was bigger, now smaller, receding back. His remaining hair clings to the sides of his skull, the rest is shaved, dull skin, gray almost, losing life, fading away.

"Hello, Henry."

"Hey, Ollie."

Lance smiles, standing just over the threshold. "Did you think about what we talked about yesterday?" Beyond the door the last students fade into the distance.

"Yes."

"And what do you think?" Lance steps closer, excited.

"Nothing."

"Nothing?" Lance sits suddenly, a child's desk, uncomfortable.

"Nothing," Henry repeats.

"What does that mean?"

"I'm not sure. Maybe I didn't think about it." Henry fiddles with a pen.

"You have to. You'll see that it makes sense. And there's more to it. I didn't tell you everything."

"Oh."

"When you really consider it, really think it through, you'll see there's a freedom to it. A sort of faith that there's a finite solution."

"The end of the world?"

"Yes and no."

"Ollie, it's Friday. I'm tired-"

"Just a moment." Lance pauses and takes a controlled breath. "Everything works, the numbers and the chaos, all your actions and my actions, all actions are part of the bigger equation. And the senseless becomes important and more than that, necessary. Instead of worrying about the desires of others, you see the larger implications. This had to happen or that had to be, because it's part of the greater whole."

"Ollie-"

"Follow the thought process, follow the formula and you don't have to worry anymore. This will happen or that won't because that's the way it should be."

"God's plan? I thought you were an atheist."

"Religion and God are as much a part of it as you and me. Don't separate them, don't make them something they're not. It's all part of the equation. War, genocide, birth, miracles, oblivion, it's all part of it."

Henry looks about his desk; the picture, the pen, the calendar.

"See it for what it is. And then you're free and your actions must take place. Even the variations are factored in, because there aren't any real variations but simple divergences of the greater computation."

"And the end of the world?"

"The world, a world, there's so many. Don't limit it."

"What's that supposed to mean?"

"You'll see and then you'll know."

"This is getting upsetting."

"Then get upset. It's all part-"

"Don't. Not again. No more equations, no more formulas, no more of this bullshit." Henry rises, overcome.

Lance also rises and moves to stop Henry. "Wait, just wait." He reaches out to Henry and touches him.

Henry looks down at Lance's hand, gray, frail, shaking slightly. "No more." He grabs his coat and brushes past the old man, leaving him alone in the room.

Epilogue to Episode 17

What if, and I'm not saying he is, but stranger things have happened, what if he's right? Maybe not right, but onto something, some ancient mystery of the universe. Some grand secret that all the geniuses and philosophers missed, but this high school teacher figured it out.

"Not now, Carter."

If not now, when? C'mon, isn't this the least bit cool? Putting all the pieces together, like those mini-series in comics.

"Life is not a comic book."

Well, not a good one. But it's certainly comic. Get it?

"Not now."

You're too serious. You can't understand the childhood joy of this idea. The guy knows the date of the end of the world. He's figured it out. Doesn't that sound awesome? And it's the loner, the guy everyone thought was insane. A bit of a cliché, but still cool. The end of the world and only he knows it. One voice in the wilderness. Epic, Hank, truly epic. And he wants to tell you. He wants you to know the end of the world.

"I can't think about that now. Too much to do."

Oh, yes, the mission. I had you pegged for quick-witted do-gooder. There's more fun in that type of character.

"Circumstances wouldn't let me."

Circumstances? Some hero you are. Punching the villain and making a joke. You know, light-hearted, tweaking society's foibles.

"Tweaking what?"

I read it once, Spider-man or Flash. Ridicule the bad guy, witty banter, that sorta thing. Not dark or brooding, hiding in the shadows, the viciousness of the attacks, truly vicious, Hank. That isn't like you at all. Bordering on madness.

"It's a mad world. Math teachers going mad."

Or letting themselves go or worse yet, making themselves go, an excuse for action.

"This isn't helping, Carter."

I'm not sure it's supposed to.

Episode 18: Angles of Light and Dark

The brightness of the day makes the afternoon commute treacherous. The perfect angle of the sun makes the world a flash. The sky is a grand and brilliant blue and the orb of yellow opens onto the world and there is nothing left hidden. The air is crisp, alive and electric. People venture out, bracing themselves, trying to encompass the world.

Henry finds his wife in the living room reading. She smiles at him, a smooth grin without vice or darkness or blight. The room is cast in a great glare as one might expect from heaven where no shadow is left to linger and all things are apparent, without sin or mystery. Everything in the room is as it is, television is television, lamp is lamp, couch is couch, and Diana is Diana. There is no double meaning, no metaphor, no symbolism, every aspect of the thing is understood, yet everything exists independently of everything else, the room itself ceases to be an eternity, and these things, this person is its or her own reality, unable or unwilling to meld. It's bright, too bright and Henry squints.

"Hello, dear. How was your day?"

"Fine."

"Hank, what is it?"

"Nothing. I can't see anything in here." He steps quickly to the kitchen, which is bright in the morning but darker in the evening, a pale gray, growing deeper.

Diana comes up behind him and wraps her arms around his chest. "Tell me."

Henry leans back, smells her, feels her eye lashes on the back of his neck, real and not real.

"Is this part of it?"

"Hmm?"

"You know, some type of amends?"

"Amends? For what?"

"For leaving? For coming back?"

She keeps hold of him and they remain together in the kitchen. "Was that wrong? Either of them?"

"I don't know."

"Why should I make amends?"

"It was wrong."

"It was?"

"Yes. You shouldn't have left."

"Why?"

Henry looks down, she's wearing the ring on her left hand. The hands are holding him tightly, pulling him into her. "It seemed wrong when you left. You didn't say goodbye."

"That's because I was coming back. If I said goodbye I couldn't have come back. I would've stayed away."

"That doesn't make sense."

"It did to me."

"Remember when I told you about Barry Jordan this morning?"

She lets him go and the connection is broken. She opens the refrigerator and pours him some juice. She went shopping. He hasn't had grape juice since she left. He drinks a full glass.

"Want more?"

He looks at the glass, faded purple, like dried blood. "How about a beer?"

"You sure?" A hint of apprehension in her voice.

"Yes, I'm fine. I just think I need a beer. Have one with me."

She opens two bottles, after finding them tucked in the back of the refrigerator. She watches Henry drink deeply. "I remember Barry," she whispers.

A faint trickle of foam spills over Henry's bottom lip. "He might be fired for hitting a kid."

"Oh." She sips.

"Yeah. I had to talk to the principal about it."

"Did he deserve it?"

"Who?"

"The kid. Did he deserve to get hit?"

"I don't know."

"Seems important." She sips again.

"Why?"

"It's important to know why. I read that. The action either becomes meaningless or more meaningful if you know why."

"I suppose so." Henry finishes his beer. "Where's Arthur?"

"Basement."

"I'll go check on him."

"I'll start dinner. We made it to the store today and I got roast beef."

Henry smiles. Diana smiles.

Arthur is sitting quietly near a section of the city known as Gotham, a distinct area noted for music and fringe culture. Home to the artistically alienated and those without art but driven to seek it, empty and wanting. People come to Gotham to explore desires labeled bohemian and adventurous, to delve into perversions exorcised from the more accepted parts of the great metropolis, such as the financial district known as Central

City. But in Gotham, where the buildings can't reach the sky, living in the shadows of Titans is the real heart of the city, the unknowable oblivion to be explored with and in some cases without restraint, to know yourself and what is and is not possible. This is the soul of all cities made of cardboard and papier-mâché, of concrete and steel, of glass and brick, designed and built by mad architects lost in their own worlds of symbols and everyday temples. Great and terrible minds created this thing, this place of imagination and space. Here on this street and on that, left of the greater whole is a true face of the city: confused, dark-eyed, breathing the fragrances of thousands of lives that have come and gone and will come again, this dark Gotham of the world.

"Hello, Arthur."

The boy's eyes are focused downward, looking and watching, the observing God, the subject of prayer and myth.

"Arthur."

There is no response from his son, but, and Henry questions its existence, not now, any time but now, when things are growing tenuous; there are slight tremors among the city: a breath, a step, a kiss, something there among the pictures of reality.

"Arthur?"

"I can hear you, Dad."

"Then say something."

"I'm sorry, but an important thing is happening."

Not now. "Arthur, are you okay? Have you been taking your pills?"

"Have you?"

"This isn't about me."

"I know, but this is important."

"What's happening?" Henry asks his son.

"I'm not exactly sure. I can only feel that's it's going to be important."

"Arthur, look at me. Are you sure you're all right? How long have you been down here?"

Arthur shuffles. "Most of the day, I think." He coughs and looks up. "It's Mrs. Grayson. She's coming to this place. She's been led here."

"She has?" Henry plays along, moving toward his son.

"She's come here, a last hope. She's heard about this place when she talked to the police. They said there's no trace of her son. That he just disappeared. She cried then, she got angry, very angry."

"Why?"

"No one just disappears she told them. There has to be some evidence. She screamed at them that her son was real, even showed them a picture of him, it was faded, taken when he was younger. She told them he had to be somewhere, it's impossible to vanish completely. There is always something she said."

"What did the police say?"

"They were sorry for her. One of them tried to hug her. She pushed him away. She was very sad and very... what's the word?"

"Desperate?"

"I think that's it. What's that mean?"

"Wanting something very badly. Wanting something more than anything else."

"Is it like love?"

"I suppose," Henry answers, standing next to his son, looking over Gotham.

"Then that's it. She loves her son, real or not. She doesn't care what people believe. A policeman who felt very sorry for her told her about this place. He said some people wind up here. He almost said people disappear here, but he didn't."

"What did she find?"

"Nothing yet, but she's getting close to the end. She feels more than the rest, but they all feel it. She's walking around and looking around. Soon she'll start asking strangers about her son."

"Where is she?"

Arthur looks up and then back at the milk cartons and the paper clip people.

"Yes, I know that would be telling." Henry leans down and kisses the top of his son's head. "Five more minutes and then come up for dinner."

Episode 19: The Mask of Righteousness

After dinner the phone rings. Diana gives it to Henry, who smiles at her. The scent of roast beef clings to the air. The world has grown dark around the house and the stars look down, casting a pall over the Earth like a multitude of light bulbs, not too bright, but enough to see the world without detail.

"Hello." Henry coughs slightly, holding his glass of wine, the bubbles bursting in his mouth.

"Evenin', Hank."

"Barry?"

"Yeah, it's me."

"What can I do for you?"

"I thought I'd call and tell you I'm resigning, but I appreciate you not telling O'Brien anything."

Another cough as the wine adds vitality to the night, making objects distinct and not distinct. "I had nothing to say."

"But you could have, that's the thing. You could have told her about how I talk about the kids, the things I say about them. But you didn't. I wanted to thank you."

"It was nothing. I would never tell her about that stuff. It was all a joke, anyway."

There is a short silence. "That's the thing. Maybe at one time it was a joke, but toward the end, it wasn't anymore. They'd gotten to me, so much that I did hate them, all of them."

"Oh."

"Maybe you're still too young or maybe you'll never get that way, but it was awful. Now I can see it, I can take a step back. It was a wretched life I was leading. So full of hate and ugliness that I couldn't break from the character I had become." There is another pause. "It was a character. It wasn't me. I wanted you to know that too. I had built this thing to protect myself, not caring, only a job and in time it took over. I became, what was in its heart a lie. I see that now."

"Barry, I-"

"Don't get upset or anything like that. This isn't part of some twelve-step program. I haven't found Jesus. I've just found out something about myself. It's more like I remember something. I became a man that I didn't want to be. And the sad fact is I didn't fight against the creation. It was easy to just fall into patterns. I did this before so I'll do it again. There was no fight on my part. I would tell myself not every man becomes who he wants to be. Life is fluid, things happen beyond your control. This leads to that and so on. And then here I was and all my energy was focused on maintaining my creation. Then it was gone. I knew I didn't want it. And I wasn't afraid of starting over."

"Barry, that's great, it really is." The wine is touching a nerve, mixing and creating a thought, "but…"

"What, Hank? What is it?"

The power comes through the phone line, through the wires and transistors, giving voice to insights, the wine letting loose. "It seems to be a new creation, doesn't it?"

"How so?"

Henry's eyes are glassy, staring off in the distance. "It's another character, as you said. Or more than that, a fantasy or coping method. You realize that all your childhood dreams, an author maybe, someone important, is now and forever falling away. You were going to be fired. That's a fact of reality that you refuse to address. A middle-aged, divorced man fired for hitting a kid. A finite conclusion to your life. As for starting over, assuming that's where you're going, it seems unrealistic. You can't start over in the middle of something. There's no erasing what's happened, so starting over is a false hope. It's going to set in, the truth of the situation, the awful reality of what it is."

"The truth of the situation?"

"Yes, the bare bones of what the world is. Your career, everything you worked for, even this personality you're rejecting now, was at one time important and now is a hollow premise, gone in an instant."

"I don't regret it."

"Maybe. And maybe a year from now you might, when there is nothing on the horizon. You'll think that this crisis point was not a great change, but bad luck, a momentary lapse and not really as important when compared to what was lost."

There's a murmur on Jordan's end. Henry sips his wine, a slight grin about his mouth, thoughts of Diana, beautiful Diana.

"See, Hank, that's the real difference between us. You see this as you want. And, as romantic as this might sound, I prefer to think of it as what it might be. I am not locked into one thing or another. I became focused, stuck in something. I've always thought the basis of life is invention. Change is necessary. Being fired, my divorce, hitting that kid were all parts of the invention and now, as you said, I'm going to start over, well not over, but start again."

"Did you hit that kid?"

"Yes. He deserved it. He said awful things about another child, truly vicious. His parents should have taught him consequences. I punched him and I feel good about it. You should understand."

Henry puts his glass down. "What?"

"Listen, I just want to thank you again. I guess, I'll see you around, but probably not. Good bye, Hank."

Henry wants to say something, regain his profundity and force Jordan to know the intricacies of the world. "Bye."

The room is quiet except for small sounds that filter in from the living room, television and comments from Diana and Arthur. Henry finishes his wine and joins them in front of the electric hearth.

"You seem content," Diana tells him.

"It's the wine. Makes my cheeks red," he responds.

She pushes him. "Don't lie. It's because I'm home."

"Home?"

"Yes."

"That's the first time you've mentioned that word."

"Home?"

"Yes. You or I used the word 'back'."

"Oh."

"It's nothing, just something I've noticed. Odd, though, that you used it now. As if something's changed."

"Oh my, you are drunk."

"No."

"You always get philosophical and deep when you're drunk."

"Hmm."

She smiles at him as she turns off the light and lays her head on his chest. "Tell me then, tell me all your theories of home and back."

He touches her head, moves her hair, thinks of a dream about a broken doll. "I'm happy you're home."

She holds him tightly and eventually they fall asleep. He dreams of an old girlfriend and how she used to hold him in his childhood bed.

Episode 20: Solitude and Caves

Hands are shaking. Can't control them. Tremors. There will be an after, when this is done.

The price is great. And every hero needs to disappear for a while, to take time away from the battle. A cave, a fortress, Detroit, the moon, a headquarters or sanctum to rest. There they can plan. There they can relax. In that privacy, quietly and apart, the hero thinks of the grand absurdity of what he or she is doing. The costume, the fight, the notion taken from childhood imagination and an overdeveloped sense of right and wrong. The duality of the life, normal and insane. They wrestle with it, a grand skirmish of self. They brood in their domain, trying desperately to know, to believe they are right and those of the remaining world are wrong. Putting themselves into the world, but not really a part of it. Fighting the impossible fight, a struggle without end and knowing, down in their heart that nothing will change, a momentary respite in the process of gluttony. Time is passing and each day adds weight, a bruise, a broken bone, younger days of healing long behind them, until that one night when they fail. And the solitude of a cave or castle will eventually turn into a tomb.

His left eye is swollen shut. The right one looks about the basement, not focusing, just moving and watching. He's not broken yet. The duct tape has fallen off his mouth, soaked through. He doesn't talk, doesn't beg. Blood has dried in his nostrils and his breaths are strained. He forces out the clot, spits it almost. His head trembles slightly. His muscles tense, he's resisting. A new piece of tape and he almost welcomes it.

Henry has retained his gym membership for the sole purpose of racquetball. Saturdays in the winter are spent in the white box, sweating with another person and nothing else but the ball and the racquet. Arthur is usually left with Henry's parents but now Diana's back. He kissed her when he left, he thought she smiled. He remembers the smell of her sleep, peaceful and wonderful.

Henry belongs to a racquetball league, twenty odd people who play on Saturday mornings, eventually crowning a champion. Henry has won it before, being slightly younger than most of the other participants. But the winning is not important, it's the isolation that registers most soundly with Henry. The apartness: no school, no Diana, nothing from his real life. A secret identity in another culture where he can play and only play. The talk is always of a shot, a ball, a racquet, or new strings. Henry smiles as he parks in the ramp and removes his equipment. Smiles and clenches against the cold. Smiles in the locker room as he stretches and smiles as he warms-up.

He anticipates the release, thrives on the abandonment to the sport, the simple, all-encompassing focus, the purity of action and of thought. Given over to the outcome, all strength, all will to the game. He tried golf, tried running, the sports appropriate to his age. But both were too expansive, too open and without proper definition. But racquetball, a box in a room, within a building, energy confined, released from within, hidden from the world was more appealing to him, more him in his imagination. And so he plays once a week, every week.

He watches the last points of the match before his own. Two older men, athletic and graceful as the years pass by. One wins and the other loses. They shake hands and leave the court. They greet Henry as he enters the room.

Henry walks the perimeter of the court, three white walls and a glass back. Small blue imperfections give the walls substance. The light seems to emanate from the whiteness of the walls. His fingers feel the warmth hanging in all parts of the court. There is no shadow in any corner.

He begins, very gently, to hit the blue ball against the front wall, taking a step back with each swing. Eventually moving back against the glass wall. Henry drives the ball forward with ferocity, unleashing the racquet, punishing the ball, put it through the wall, right through and beyond. Sweat forms on his arms, a good sweat from exertion, nothing ignoble about it, no fear in it. The back door opens and his opponent steps onto the court.

She's tall, her legs disappearing into blue shorts. She wears a red top, sports bra beneath, evident, there to be seen or she doesn't care. Confident. Her hair is pulled back and she wears a yellow headband. She's strong, muscular, her eyes are hidden beneath goggles.

"Hello, I'm Linda," she tells him. Soft voice, quiet, inward.

"Hello," Henry stammers, an unexpected reaction. Not intimidated, concerned perhaps, interested, different.

"This is my first match. I just joined the league. Something else to do in the winter, I suppose."

"Yeah," Henry whispers.

"I'm not a novice, though. I played in college, so I know what I'm doing. I don't want you to think that this is a waste of your time. I'll give you a game."

"I'm sure."

"Mind if we hit together?" she asks.

Henry bounces the ball and taps it against the wall, which Linda returns. He watches her, she's focused on each shot, but effortless, natural athlete, comfortable and graceful. She hits harder, raising the intensity. Henry follows her lead. A rhythm forms, something that can be known and understood on an instinctual level, a heartbeat, a life of thump and swish, the air parted by racquet and ball.

"I'm ready to start. Are you?" Linda asks. The echo of the ball drowns out her voice, but Henry knows the question and nods.

He serves first. The anticipation grows, the sweat feels right and he smiles, bounces the ball twice, pulls the racquet back and the game begins. The match starts awkwardly, missed shots, easy shots not made, sloppy and without crisp movement, unsure as novice lovers are. But then, midway through the first game, best of five, it happens, the resurfacing of rhythm, unspoken, but understood through movement and competition. Shot and counter shot, a point and another. Some are remarkable, decisive kill shots and measured angle shots. Linda proves to be an impressive opponent, gliding to the ball, barely a movement and the ball is off the wall and Henry must compensate, skipping it off the opposing wall, solid and precise. Soft grunts mix with the sounds of crash, bang, and wallop. They don't talk but nod, acknowledging a superb shot, an effort seldom seen in the muted world of adult sports, which is defined by waning youthful energy, competition relegated to small intimate affairs and quick glimpses of caring.

The fifth game proves the most contested, lasting well past the twenty-one-point limit. Winning by two becomes a grand accomplishment. Each competitor serves, each returns, pushing each other, forcing the opponent to do more, to be more. A bond is nurtured between the white walls and glass back. The final point is struck and they exhale, full and empty, euphoric and exhausted, they smile.

Out of the box, Henry tries to latch onto the feeling that was created within the white confines for just a few minutes more. "Nice game."

"And you," Linda replies.

"Can I offer you a drink? A trophy for the winner."

"Sure, why not?" Linda smiles.

They walk to the juice bar, Henry following her, sweat clinging to her shoulders. He orders and she orders, and they sit. An awkward silence pervades. The invitation was well intentioned, but now what to say? How to start? Linda wipes her face and drinks.

"I know you don't I? From somewhere?" she asks.

"I'm not sure. What's your last name again?"

"Forsythe."

"Oh." The name is familiar, but he can't place it. "No, I mean it sounds familiar, but I'm not sure."

She drinks lemon infused water. "Are you a teacher?"

Surprised slightly, Henry responds, "Yes."

"That's probably it. I used to work for a local school district."

"Oh," Henry sputters grape infused water.

"Did you ever play in the annual golf tournament?"

"Yes. You were there?"

"Shocking, I know. I finished first for the women the last time I played, being the only woman."

"That's right. I remember. You didn't get your award. A wise ass ran up and made a joke and took your trophy. Did you ever get it back?"

"No. It doesn't matter." Her voice drops an octave.

"So what are you doing now?" Henry asks.

"Hmm?" She comes back from a far off place.

"You said you worked for a district, but not anymore?"

"No, not anymore. Something happened."

"Oh." Henry leans back, the comradeship dissipating in the air between.

"It's a sordid tale. And I feel I'm boring if I tell it all the time. I don't want to be boring."

"Well, as a stranger, if I thought you were boring I would never tell you. It would be rude," Henry says with a grin.

109

"Very noble of you. To put it bluntly, a man, a friend asked me to raise his daughter and I felt obliged to accept. She has special needs so I don't have time to work. The job was quickly becoming dull anyway."

"That's very nice of you, to raise someone else's child."

"I suppose. I'm still not used to it. My cousin is watching her now. You need some time to yourself."

"Yeah, my son can be a handful."

"Suffer the little children."

They both drink.

"Now, you must tell me something interesting about you," she says and looks into his eyes. "I shared and you should also. But nothing too deep. If we play again, you can't give me any ammunition for psychological warfare."

"Okay." Henry thinks for a moment. He watches Linda smile, anticipating something. "A friend told me the other day that he knew when the world was going to end. He said it's going to happen soon."

Linda looks askance at Henry. "Really?"

"Oh yes. He seemed quite sure."

"Hmm. Well, that is interesting. How does this person know?"

"A formula, math. He's a Math teacher, so am I. He's figured out the date that the world is going to end."

"Is he right?"

"I don't know."

"Seems important. Check his figures. See if there's a mistake."

"I guess."

"Look to it."

Henry drinks. "Is this how people react when they hear that someone's figured out when the world will end?"

"How are people supposed to react?"

"It's insane. Don't you think it's insane?"

"I never met the man, so I can't say. Do you think he's crazy?"

"No. But now I'm not sure."

"What if every crackpot and scheme, every idea called madness had within them a kernel, a nucleus of truth and was only lacking the connective element, the line that connects them all together. All that's missing is the key."

"You sound like my friend. All that's missing in the equation is the starting point."

"Maybe he's on to something."

"Maybe, but I doubt it."

"It's easier to dismiss it, I suppose, to call it insanity."

"Easier or he is insane. A reflection of his own inner turmoil. The end of his own world is the end of the world."

"A dark love..."

"What?"

"Nothing."

They drink again, sitting forward, finding themselves closer. Linda looks at her infused water deeply, touching the plastic bottle as if might be something incredibly precious, something rare and beautiful. Her voice is soft when she begins talking. "Is the dark desolation of a world on the brink of the abyss so much more than one soul, one mind facing that same eternal question daily or hourly? The fighting not to jump as an individual is so much more dramatic than a world bent on self-destruction. A world dying is nothing compared to the loneliness of being."

"Huh?"

"Sorry." She looks up at Henry, an expression passing from her face. "I've been morose of late. A symptom, I suppose, of becoming a parent."

"How so?"

"Seeing the child, wanting good things to happen, but knowing, based on your own life, that goodness goes hand in hand with tragedy. There's a temperance to raising children I've found. A woman told me once that you are your children. If that's true you have to be worried."

"I guess it is true."

"This woman also told me that you can lose yourself in your children. That's why I joined this league. I join things to keep myself from becoming my child."

"Never thought of it that way." Henry finishes his fruit water.

"Maybe this is what's wrong with your friend, assuming there is something wrong with him. Does he have a family?"

"He was married. I'm not sure he has children."

"Not that close?" Linda asks.

Henry shakes his head and fidgets with his empty bottle.

"Doesn't matter," Linda says and smiles. "But think of it. Your friend's world collapsed either due to action or inaction. So he creates this theory to compensate for his life or the path his life has taken. If the world ends, then his life ends and his mistakes, his tragedies are meaningless against the greater tragedy of the end of the universe."

Linda gazes at the people who now play in the white room. Two more bodies moving in rhythm with purpose.

"Then what's left?" Henry asks.

She pauses, taking a sip from her beverage. "Love, I want to answer. Love lasts forever, so I've been told. But it's difficult to believe. Faith I guess. Faith is something that keeps us going. Faith the sun will rise and your friend is wrong. It's funny, faith in the fallibility of others."

"Yeah," Henry whispers, forcing a smile.

"One man's death is the crumbling of the world. I've seen it. And the tragedy is monumental. The end of the world or the end of a world, no difference in the end. Numbers, I suppose, one versus the multitude, one in contrast to billions. There's nothing earth shaking in one. I think we want it to be more than it is. We make it more in our own imagination. But to witness the decay, first-hand, see it, touch it, there is no comparison. One versus billions. One is far more important and the other is used for statistics."

"That's rather morbid."

"I'm sorry. I do that from time to time. Drift in my own stream of thought. Perhaps we can talk about the weather."

"Hmm." Henry feels uncomfortable and pulls back slightly.

"Too deep for a Saturday. So I'll take my leave. It was nice to meet you and talk." She gathers her belongings.

"It was a pleasure."

"Perhaps I'll see you again in the playoffs." Linda smiles a wry grin.

"Only if I'm lucky."

They shake hands and part ways. Henry sits again and watches a match between two older men. The shots are more precise than his own, no opportunity escapes. Movement is measured as age will not allow for sprints or any prolonged physical exertion, no rally over five hits. They smile and talk to each other. It's not too serious, not overly important who wins. Each day is a gift, precious and to be taken into account against the backdrop of war and famine and the gross discontent of humanity. Henry tries shut his power down, receiving too much: angst over a body that won't get smaller, capturing youth, a comment taken to heart, pushing and pushing, freedom, a dream of being a professional, ritual, the filling of something, she'll say yes now, I look better now, heartbreak in the past, he'll say yes now, it's all worth it in the end. Henry closes his eyes and walks to the locker room.

"How was your game?" Diana asks. She is sitting in the living room with Arthur, cutting milk cartons into the shapes of buildings.

"Fine."

"Did you win?"

"No."

"Well, maybe next time."

"Maybe."

She smiles up at him while Arthur remains consumed by his construction.

"I had this really intense conversation with the woman I played against."

"Intense how?" Diana asks as she hands the glue to Arthur.

"I told her about the end of the world. We talked about Ollie's theory."

"You seem rather obsessed by that."

"No, not really. But it's fascinating. This woman didn't even blink when I mentioned it. She picked up on the idea and talked about it."

"What did you expect?"

"I'm not sure. Something else, I guess. When a stranger tells you the world is going to end, it seems you would change the subject, talk about something else."

"Hmm." Diana cuts and glues.

Henry walks to the kitchen and fills a glass with water. Outside the sun is shining through the clouds. The whiteness of the snow intensifies, but will only grow dark again as clouds pass above the house. The phone rings.

"New buildings, something new to look at, show that things are fine, getting better even." Arthur carries his new buildings to the basement, Diana trailing behind him.

"That's what people want?" she asks.

"They're not sure. But this might help. New things are good."

Diana pauses to look at Henry. His face seems pale. "What is it?" she asks.

"My dad. He's in the hospital. He's had a heart attack."

Episode 21: The Dark Hand of the Lady

The room smells of antiseptic. Henry's mother is sitting next to her husband. She smiles at her son's approach.

"Hello, Hank."

"Mom, is he…"

Henry's father lies quietly, his are eyes shut and tubes and IV bags hang about him. His skin is pale and his chest rises and falls with a pump located on the wall. A machine beeps at regular intervals.

"The doctors aren't sure. They want him stable before they run more tests. It's more than likely he's suffered a heart attack that may have triggered a stroke. They're not going to do any more tests until tomorrow." Henry's mother looks at her husband. Her voice is quiet, factual, without an excess of emotion.

"When did this happen?"

"Early this morning. He was rigid and couldn't breathe. I called the ambulance. He's been in the emergency room until an hour ago."

Henry advances and touches his father's hand. It's warm, hot almost, life yet. He reaches out; panic, peace, confusion and clarity, all jumbled. He pulls back.

"It's all right, Hank."

Henry looks at his mother, soft in the dim lights, sitting and watching.

"Are Arthur and Diana here?" she asks.

"They're in the lobby. I wanted to know Dad's condition before I brought them up. I don't think Arthur should see his grandfather like this."

"It might be the last time," she says, matter of fact, nothing harsh about it, plain and simple. "But then again, you may be right," she adds.

Henry nods. "I'll go get them."

He passes nurses and doctors, faceless people who live and work amongst misery and potential death. He finds his son and wife sitting in the lobby.

"How about that one?"

"No."

"That one?"

"No."

"That one?"

"No."

"That one?"

"I'll know when I see the person."

Diana has her arm around Arthur, as the boy holds his camera.

"It has to be natural, like they don't know I'm taking their picture. Sometimes I have to wait a long while for the right one."

"I see," Diana responds.

Henry watches them from the vestibule, sitting next to each other as people walk past. The lobby is busy and sickness is everywhere. Diana nudges Arthur who shakes his head. She smiles. Henry eventually takes the seat next to her.

"He's in a room on the sixth floor. My mother is there."

"How is he doing?" she asks.

"They're not sure yet. More tests tomorrow."

"So there's no prognosis?"

"Maybe a heart attack and a stroke."

"Goodness." She looks at Arthur.

"We can go see him," Henry whispers.

"Why?"

Henry pauses. "I thought Arthur might…"

"Oh, yes, yes. Take him up and I'll wait here."

"You won't come?"

"No, I think it's best I stay here."

"Why?"

"Nothing really. It should just be you and your mother and Arthur. I should stay here."

"Okay."

Henry takes Arthur by the hand and leads him to the elevators. They wait and board with five other people. Arthur watches the people, taller than he, trees with branches and moving roots. His perspective allows him to note minor imperfections in dress, a frayed belt, torn pants. The faces remain obscured, unknowable at their height, but the rest, the trunks reveal stories and tales. Ragged fingernails, a cell phone buzzing and ignored, mismatched socks, a lab coat neatly pressed, fidgeting, tapping of a pen. Arthur watches it all.

In front of his father's room, Henry crouches before his son. "Now, Grandpa's in bed and looks very different. There are tubes and wires, and he doesn't look like himself. I don't want you to be scared."

"I'm not scared," Arthur replies.

"That's good."

"Are you scared, Dad?"

Henry watches his son's gray eyes, almost blue at the edges, and then his gaze moves to his son's small nose like Diana's, thin mouth like Diana, a look of concern like Diana. "No, everything is fine."

Henry's mother hugs her grandson as he enters. Arthur moves to the bed and stands on his tiptoes to see. Henry moves next to his mother. They stand quietly, vigil-like. Henry sees the funeral, himself and his mother in a similar state of repose. He almost cries suddenly, overcome with the image.

Arthur touches his grandfather's hand. He takes note of the details; trimmed nails, a smell similar to the cleaner his mother uses in the kitchen, faint white hair on the knuckles, a faded wedding ring, tarnished, slight needle marks on the skin, purple and red. The eyes are shut tightly, breathing tube, drool at the corners of the mouth, stain on the pillow. Slowly he lifts his camera and takes a picture. The noise of the camera startles Henry.

"Arthur?"

"Just a picture," the boy responds.

"Okay. Mom, I'll take him back down and then I'll be right back. Can I get you something?"

"No, I'm fine." She sits again, chair nearest the window.

Henry takes Arthur back down the elevator, back to the lobby. Diana is there waiting.

"Is everything all right?" she asks.

"Yes. Can you take him home? I'm going to stay."

"Yes, that's best." She kisses Henry gently. She steps back and looks at him, dark eyes, haunting. "Did you know the principal that got shot last year, the hero, he's in this hospital?"

"Hmm."

"I guess he's on the same floor as your dad. I heard two nurses talking about him."

"Really?" Henry thinks of the word hero.

"I read his wife's book, coping and self-help. It's good." She takes Arthur's hand and walks away. She looks back once and then she is out the door. Henry returns to the elevators.

Episode 22: The Question is a Hero

Henry's mother is standing in the hall. He watches her as he approaches. She's looking at her left hand, Kleenex in her right. She's transfixed, staring at the rough skin, the blood and bone beneath. She is unaware of the world about her, content and displaced, adrift.

"What is it?" Henry asks.

"Changing the tubes. Be a few minutes."

Henry nods and leans against the wall. "Diana said the hero principal is here. The one in a coma."

"Yes, I know, down the hall there."

Henry looks down the hall, the rooms seemingly exactly alike. There is no sign, no marker to denote the principal's existence. "Seems lonely."

"Old news, I guess."

"Hmm."

Henry strolls, compulsion, down the hall. He pauses at rooms with people moaning and people dying, people recovering and those almost ready to be free. Nurses nod to him and he smiles. He pauses before the hero principal's door, his name written in marker on an index card taped to the door. The man who risked his life for students a short time ago and then was shot and almost died, now lies quietly in a dim room, not unlike Henry's father. Henry puts his hand on the door and moves it slightly, not really thinking, but simply moving. He steps into the room.

The bed is pushed to the corner, three chairs are placed around it, like an altar. The blinds are drawn, making the room dark, a cocoon. Henry steps further in and shuffles to the bedside. The man is motionless, except for the ventilator, pushing air into his lungs, the beep and hum of life. He's older than Henry, gray hair, wrinkles embedded in his forehead. Around his mouth a tube is taped, keeping it open.

Henry sits down next to the bed and gazes at the man. The newspapers called him a hero because of his grand and selfless gesture, a true hero, the word's simplest and greatest definition.

"I'm trying to build this up in my head. I want it to be Superman and Jor-El, Peter Parker and Uncle Ben, inspiration and the inspired. You're a hero, right? That's what you're called. I've been thinking about heroes of late. My cousin and I used to talk about heroes when we were young. He would make long speeches about the aspects of heroes and villains. I thought they were brilliant. I wonder what you would think of him. You being an actual hero and all. But you got shot. That's not supposed to happen to heroes, at least not the iconic ones. Superman died once, but didn't really die."

Henry leans over the hero principal and looks at him. His skin is pale, but alive in a technical sense.

"I'm trying to be heroic. But it's difficult to really do it. Your situation was different. You reacted, it happened and then you were facing down a gunman. Was it a conscious choice? Did you think it through? Did you find inspiration from comic books? That's silly, I suppose. My dad might die. People die. I wasn't ready for it. I guess no one is ready for that sort of thing. Still, it's affecting me. Pushing me one way or another. Then the world might end and I should be heroic. I'm worried about my dad."

Henry turns away from the hero quickly. The television is on, news about a conflict on the other side of the world. People are dying, some quickly and others slowly. Their tragedy is incomprehensible. The television shows bodies and toys in the street, oddly posed corpses covered in dirt and tainted blood, smoke in the background, giant plumes from a devastated building, and more explosions and gunfire. The voice-over tells of numbers, symbols to represent people and the lives they lost, like a math problem.

Henry turns back to the hero principal. "It seems plausible and that's frightening. The end of the world. But then a heroic example seems more important in the face of oblivion. But what if the world doesn't end? Or does? Do the things we do matter? Do you matter? Does my dad? Am I mad? I have a history. That's how I'll be remembered. I won't be a hero."

The television draws Henry's attention again. A commentator has appeared explaining that the conflict is a long-lasting process. Many people will die in the future, a forgone conclusion, already understood, already a number, you will die and you and you and you.

"But it's what I believe, isn't it? My motives aren't important to anyone else but me. I'm doing what needs to be done. Like all heroes, before their time. If you could stop Hitler before World War II, would you? It's an old question. The hero is always the lone voice. That's why they're remembered."

Henry shifts in his acolyte chair. He feels his face, stubble and slight sweat. He thinks of the racquetball game and his opponent, the sad woman with the sad ideas. She, like the rest, needs a hero, something to believe in, to make everything all right. He thinks he'd like talk with her again.

"Hello."

Henry turns. The source of the voice is standing in the doorway. She's small and delicate in the artificial light of the room. Her hair is in pigtails and she's wearing a sweater emblazoned with a reindeer. She's holding the hand of an adult, her mother, Henry guesses. She's a thin woman, dressed

121

neatly, prim and proper. She's wearing glasses, like her daughter. They seem distorted mirror images of each other.

"Hello," Henry responds.

"Can we help you?" the mother asks.

Henry stands.

"Do you know my husband?" she asks.

"No, yes, well not really." Henry smiles at the little girl. "I guess I'm a fan."

"Oh." The woman looks down at her daughter. "Did you come to see him?"

"No, I mean, yes. That is, my father is here also, down the hall. I heard your husband was here and I guess... I'm terribly sorry for interrupting you."

She smiles. "Please, I'm just happy you're not a reporter. They're have been so many."

"I'm a teacher."

"Well, that's better then. Please, sit."

"I don't want to disturb you."

"That's all right. I don't mind. A chance to talk to someone who isn't a doctor or a nurse."

All three take their places around the bed. The young girl, the daughter takes the chair closest to her father, protective posture. Henry's power is working. But the woman, the mother, his power passes through her, a void, like she isn't there. Henry crosses his legs, uncomfortable in his chair.

"My name is Melissa, by the way. This is my daughter."

"My name is Henry Kent. It's very nice to meet you both." Henry smiles at the little girl, who returns the facial expression.

"Nice to meet you, too, Henry. Tell me, why did you want to see my husband?"

She's focused, not looking away, but still aware of her husband, come to terms with his condition. Henry remembers seeing her picture on the back of Diana's book.

"My father is in a room down the hall. I needed a walk, get out for a moment. I recognized your husband. I also heard the nurses talking about him."

"Of course. I hope it's not serious about your father," she replies, sitting back.

"Stroke. As to what the actual prognosis is, I'm not sure."

"Sickness is difficult on those who can only watch."

"I suppose so," Henry responds.

She smiles suddenly, her daughter is also smiling. "My husband was fond of that phrase: I suppose so."

"Hmm."

"No one can predict the future, Henry. We can only take the things as they come. Prepare ourselves for happiness and sadness. It's the way of life."

"Is that from your book?" Henry asks, uncrossing his legs.

"You know it?"

"My wife is reading it."

"That's nice. Thank her for me."

"I will."

They're quiet for a moment. Henry thinks about what she said. He asks, "Is that the key, preparation?"

"There is no key, no real key. It's a bad metaphor, locks and such, like we're trying to escape from something, get out as it were."

"Never thought of it that way."

"But preparation is part of the process, the whole evolution of a life. It's sad to say or even cold, but people die, Henry. This is known. One cannot escape death. But one can prepare. Through understanding and an honest view of the world, death ceases to be traumatic."

"No offense, but that does seem cold." Henry glances at the hero principal.

"Yes, yes. I've been accused of that. It's been a major criticism of my book. But if one investigates death, and I use it only as an example, as it is the obsession with so many, the idea of dying has been the basis of many rituals and motivations for action. Why do we feel bad when someone dies? Billions believe in an afterlife. The idea of life after death dates back to the beginning of mankind. If these places, life after death, exist, why do we fear death?"

"That's a point, I guess."

"The trouble is there is no absolute knowledge of an afterlife. Faith comes into play. For if there were certainty, then this life would be meaningless and people would have no qualms about doing awful things, for there would be something better on the other side. But with doubt you have a modicum of control." She pauses and leans forward. "But what if this is it? Then what?"

Henry watches her speak, the fervor tempered by her reserved nature. Henry sees the strength in her, the hidden understanding of the world. The void that hides her from his power is punctured here and there, and what is revealed is glorious. "I'm not sure."

"Sorry about that, Henry. I didn't mean to talk at you."

Like dusk, the shroud again descends over the author and his power can no longer reach her. "That's quite all right. I enjoyed it."

She smiles at him, wry and quick. "Preparation is only one way of coping. But coping with disasters, death, depression, loss in the largest sense, is the main function of society. Either good or bad, we cope and attempt to move on."

"That sounds cruel, but I see your point."

"Well, in my opinion, coping is the highest achievement allowed by society. Handling the great good and the great bad. Knowing that this or that must end, grieving or rejoicing. It's the best that anyone can do in the end."

"And everything ends?"

"I'm afraid so, Henry."

"Even the world will end."

Melissa, wife and mother and author, nods. "Everything."

They sit again in silence. The little girl watches Henry. He smiles at her. In time he rises, thanks the author, waves to the little girl and departs.

The hall is quiet, a nurse here and there. Henry pauses before his father's door and then enters.

Episode 23: The Answer is a Villain

When I shut my eyes and open them again, I think what if this time he's not there and all of this is just a dream. But then I hear him breathing and moaning. His sounds fill the room. The softer the noise, the more it penetrates me. The power drill drowns them out.

A hero needs a confidant, a person who knows but does not judge, an anchor to the reality of the world. All the great ones had this trustee. Whether it be a butler, a lover, a wife, a parent, even a sidekick; they are all a person to care about beyond the overall quest for justice. Of course this person is put in great peril, knowing a secret makes one a target. Yet no hero can survive without this outlet for frustration and desperation. Although the ultimate loner is the superhero, no one can be utterly alone. The nature of the hero is secretive. Sure there are groups, heroes who band together, but nothing is as sacred as the powerless confidant. Of particular interest is the example of the lover. The added dimension of physical love, the bond that must exist, opens a myriad of problems and possible plot lines. But it also leads to what's referred to as 'The Ultimate Showdown'. Death then is always a part of the lover scenario. Perhaps the best confidants are those who are already dead.

You could tell me things now. All the terrible things you've done or thought about doing. You could tell me and I would listen. The darkness that you thought of, the crimes you've conceived in your bedroom. There are no secrets between us now. Would you like me to start? Shall I tell you something about my father?

Henry's father's room is quiet as he pauses at the threshold. His mother sits next to the bed reading, her hand on her husband's shoulder. Henry can see the snow falling through the window.

"Hello, Henry." His mother's voice is even.

"Hi, Mom. Any change? What did the doctors say?"

"Nothing. They told me about more tests they plan to run tomorrow, but they seemed confused as to what to do next."

"Hmm."

"Do you mind sitting here for a moment? I need to get something to drink and make a phone call."

"Sure."

"Thank you, dear." She kisses him on the cheek and brushes past him and out the door.

Henry surveys the room and decides he is uncomfortable. His breaths have become short, as if he's afraid to fill his lungs, afraid to choke, cough, or die. The room is warm, innocuous with the surrounding winter. Vapors of heat filter through the air, fogging the windows around the edges. Henry's skin feels dry, like paper, hurtful, capable of being torn, but there would be no blood beneath, only dust, a fine powder that would flee on the warm air currents, dispersed as if it were never solid, never alive. Henry winces. He pulls a chair closer to his father and sits.

"You look different, Dad. Vulnerable, I guess. I've seen you emotionally vulnerable before. That was... well, to be blunt, upsetting. I was ashamed of you, how you reacted to Mom's departure. Huh, flight and departure." Henry smiles for a moment. "But she came back. And Diana came back. You were right about them. Or maybe, you just got lucky. We got lucky."

A machine buzzes.

"To be done in like this? Hooked to wires, struggling to breathe. It's hollow. Not heroic at all. I'm sorry to say that, dad. I started talking about you and I move to myself. Selfish, I suppose, but I have to talk someone. Carter was right about the confidant. You remember Carter, don't you? You used to take us to get comic books every week. Remember the other boy who was always in the store? Dan was his name. There is a point to this, Dad. Sometimes I wonder whatever became of Dan. I suppose he became something or maybe he didn't. But that's the point. He was part of my make-up, my origin. I saw him every week for about five years. He's part of my equation. He was a morose kid, but he would talk with Carter and me about comics, plot lines, who should die and such. He said something once that has stayed with me all these years. We were talking about killing off major characters and he said the destiny of a character is already written, but that destiny changes with each new writer and there's always a new writer."

A commotion in the hallway causes Henry to look up as nurses rush past.

"That's interesting, don't you think? I thought it was when Dan said it. It's kind of haunted me since. I've always questioned who the writers were. God? Humans? Parents? Society? Perhaps they all are, and perhaps none are. I bring this up because I just met a writer. She told me things always end. Maybe even the writers come to an end. I heard about the end of the world."

Henry pauses as a machine beeps.

"I suppose everyone has their own theories or their own insights of the world. I have my own. It's tied to justice, right and wrong. The point I'm trying to make is you."

The machine beeps again.

"You believed Mom would come back. You were bitter and angry and pathetic and devoted. Even in your depression, probably crying, you never doubted that she would come back. And she did. All these other theories, even mine, are clung to in quiet resolve, a dignified, hidden faith. But you, there was no inner strength, only outward blubbering. You were so quick to anger, hated the world even. But you were right. Even when everyone told you to give up. Even when your own son abandoned you. You stayed true."

A nurse enters and smiles at Henry. She checks the IV bags connected to his father and departs.

"I suppose all great men had doubts. It takes great strength, superhuman strength to push beyond those doubts. That's what I have to do. The inner struggle must be more arduous than the outward. The heartfelt doubt that has no voice is far more frightening than any exposed pain. And it is the pain, you see, that is the driving force. It's all blatant, the tremendous amount of anguish we feel. The news spouts about it daily. Stories of the grand pain of the world. You know, war, conflict, bombings from on high, suicide bombers, explosions and the aftermath. Bodies lying in the streets like deer carcasses, the obvious death and destruction. But there's other pain, the more personal agonies of those around us. I feel that, honestly, I feel all of it." Henry looks away slowly. He cringes, almost as if the floodgates opened for an instant. "It's not my imagination. I'm not overly sensitive."

Another hum and air fills Henry's father's lungs.

"What can one man do? One man can save one person and one man can save the world, even if it is going to end."

Henry's mother returns and hands her son a can of soda. "I thought you might need something to drink," she says. "Were you talking to someone?"

Henry looks up at her. He notices her smooth face, gray eyes, and thin nose. He has seen pictures of her when she was young and beautiful. "No. Thanks for the soda."

"Has there been any change?"

"No. A nurse came in, nothing else."

"I suppose we'll just wait and see."

Henry opens his soda and drinks. "It's all we can do."

Henry's mother takes the seat opposite him. They sit for a time in silence. The wind blows and the machines hum.

"Mom," Henry begins quietly, "why did you come back?"

She looks up from her book and pauses before venturing an answer. "I guess it seemed like the next thing to do."

"You guess?"

"Perhaps that's the wrong phrase. It's what I had to do next."

"Destiny?"

"No, I don't care for those words, fate, destiny, even chance. Things happen and that's all. I left then I came back."

"Are you talking about whims? Is it all simply a whim?" Henry's voice rises in volume.

"Yes and no. I don't think there's a greater power out there, pushing us one way or another. Thousands of variables factor into each decision, but that decision is still a choice. I left because I chose to and I came back because I chose to. That's all."

"What if Dad didn't take you back?"

"That was his choice."

Henry looks at his father, tubes and wires and flesh and blood. "He knew you were coming back."

Henry's mother looks back to her book. "I'm sure he did."

"You hurt him, leaving like you did."

She looks at her husband. "I know. I asked his forgiveness and he forgave me."

"That's all he could do."

"Henry," she starts, looking at him patiently, "you were always concerned with reasons. But sometimes, most times the reason a person does something only makes sense to that person. To the rest of the world it's a mystery. It's just part of life."

Henry watches her. "Still, your reasons for leaving and returning, you didn't tell him did you?"

"Yes, I did. I doubt he understood. It was enough that I came back."

Henry sits back in his chair and looks out the window to the swirling snow that obscures the world. "I should get going." He rises and steps to the door.

His mother also stands and takes him by the hands. She kisses him. "I'll see you tomorrow," she says.

Henry smiles. "I believe you." They embrace and Henry leaves.

Outside the world is soft. Gray snow clouds reflect the lights of the hospital. People smile at him. Buildings are decorated merrily. Henry trudges through the snow and drives home.

Episode 24: Canaries and Arrows

Henry finds Diana in bed reading. "How's your dad?" she asks.

"Nothing new." He takes off his shirt. "Where's Arthur?"

"He fell asleep almost as soon as we got home. The hospital must have been too much for him."

"Early," Henry whispers.

"What's that?"

"Nothing. I'm tired too. Long day."

"Hmm."

"What are you reading?" Henry asks.

"I was inspired to re-read the book by the wife of the hero principal."

Henry puts on his pajamas and climbs into bed. "I met her today."

"Really? What's she like?"

"Nice. She was very nice. A bit intense, but nice." Diana seems to want more, but Henry closes his eyes. "How's the book?"

"I thought it would be a bunch of crap, positive self-image and coping, that type of nonsense. But it's actually very interesting. She doesn't drone on and on about her husband. He's only mentioned a few times. It's more psychological."

"Yeah?"

"You should read it." Diana smiles at him, across the space that separates them.

Henry opens his eyes. "Do you think I need help?"

"No, it's not like that."

"What's it like?"

She pauses and looks intently at Henry. "You want to know why I came back?"

"Yes."

"Why?"

"Why what?"

"Why do you want to know?"

"What?"

She looks into the darkness of the room. The reading lamp on her side of the bed casts the only light. "You think it'll make you happy. You think knowing will make some positive impact on your life. You think you'll be happy."

"Maybe," Henry whispers.

"You won't, though. Her big point in the book is the search for happiness is... how did she put this?" Diana flips through the pages. "Here it is. 'All our plans for happiness are empty dreams.'"

"That's depressing."

"No, you're thinking about it terms of social happiness, that happiness we think we're entitled to. But that's not happiness. She says in the book that the want for happiness dates back to ancient man. That want itself is a basic human survival instinct. And happiness is tied to ultimate survival."

Henry sighs. "I just want to know why you came back if you had to leave in the first place. I don't really care how the answer will make me feel."

She leans over and kisses him. "I came back to be happy."

Henry looks at her and she moves closer. "That's it?" he asks.

"The pursuit of happiness has always fascinated me. The notion of pursuit, run it down, chase it, movement. It made sense that happiness is not stationary. She says in the book, 'Ask yourself if you are happy and often the answer is no. The question makes you suspect that you are in fact unhappy.' That's true. I would sit here in the house and ask myself if I was happy and I could always answer, I could be happier."

"And that's why you left? Without a word? Without even talking to me about how you felt?"

"I couldn't talk to you about it."

"Why not?"

"Because of who you are. Your intelligence makes you different. I couldn't really understand it before, before I read this. Intelligence is tied to melancholy. She's done the research. She quotes a man named Burton who attempted to cure people of being melancholy." Diana flips the pages again, stopping on a page with multiple underlined passages. "In his attempt to cure melancholy, Burton found the higher the intelligence the more paralyzing the disease. These people, those with the higher intelligence, were almost incapable of being happy for more than a few seconds. To Burton's surprise a few of these 'abandoned, emotionally destitute persons' as he called them, considered happiness a mental disorder. A true human being, with a world understanding, could never be happy."

"That's really depressing."

"Don't make fun. This book is partly why I went to that religious retreat."

"You read this book before you left?"

"Just before." She smiles at him through the soft light. "So many people find happiness in religion. Happiness as a divine gift and all that. But sometimes only bestowed after death. I wanted to see if that were true, divinity and happiness. She gives examples of martyrs who were tortured and died horribly, but happily. But I didn't find happiness in religion. Maybe the divine are the only ones who are happy."

"Perhaps happiness doesn't exist."

Diana touches his hand. "No, I'm sure it does. Elements of happiness are all around us. For me, I needed to look, to search, as I said the pursuit was the most important aspect."

Henry caresses her hand, his body close to hers. "And that's why you came back?"

She slumps in the bed, placing her face next to his. She allows the book to fall to the floor. "There was a passage in her book. She was quoting a French philosopher who was touring America in the 1800's. He said, 'Every instant they think they will catch it, and each time it slips through their fingers. They see it close enough to know its charms, but they do not get near enough to enjoy it, and they will be dead before they have fully relished its delight.' That stayed with me when I was away. The tantalizing aspect of being fully happy. It's alluring and petrifying."

"Are you leaving again?"

She kisses him and pulls him close and whispers in his ear, "I can't tell, but if I do, I might take you and Arthur with me."

"I may still love you."

"I know."

She kisses him again. Her lips taste of winter's warmth, manufactured, but still deep and wonderful. She smiles. "And now, do have anything to tell me?"

He kisses her and holds her tightly. "Not tonight."

Diana is gentle, hovering above him. She smiles, he can tell, even in the darkness. They connect again as they did all those years ago, when he wasn't sure about her, when he didn't know what she was going to do next, when his power didn't work. He's ready for the end of the world. He is ready to accept the end, with her, finally again. She feels warm, her skin, her breath. They move together as if they had never been separated. This is them, he tells her, this is them apart from the world. She responds with a whisper and a kiss. He repeats himself, this is them and the rest can fade away. He pulls her close, kisses her again and tastes the sweetness of the world.

Episode 25: The Bright Blue and Red of the Sky

I sit in front of him, watching, noting the details. He has a small nose and full lips. He looks back at me, perhaps noting the details of my face. I must look terrible to him, his blood on my skin. He doesn't turn away.

The hero, apart from the relationships with any confidant, must have a bond with his nemesis, that archenemy that is at the center of the hero's world. This person is vital to the hero's story line. This arch villain comes in various shapes, from the exact opposite to the eerily similar, but whatever the villain looks like, it's what the villain represents, that darker personality of the hero and of all people that makes a truly iconic bad guy. A really great villain, a true arch foe becomes as or even more important than the hero. It's rare that the villain becomes the center of the story, but it remains one of the most interesting types of storytelling. It raises many intriguing questions. Does the villain see himself as a villain? What is his ultimate goal? Does the villain know his actions harm others? Is the villain mad? Another interesting aspect of the arch villain development is that of the hero who has turned bad. Point of view is crucial when developing an arch villain. The writer tells the story through the character and based on the author the audience knows heroes and villains. The best stories are the ones where the hero and villain are clearly defined. You know who to root for. There's no guessing, no doubt as to the outcome. The hero is going to win and that's how the story ends. The other stories, the ones that are unclear, those are harder to like. I don't care for those types of stories, when things are left unresolved.

We're nearing the end. He knows it. He's resolved to fight it. I admire that. I thought he would be weak at the end. I thought he would've given up a long time ago. After the bat or the screwdriver or the hammer. He screamed and cried but he never gave in, not like his friends, like those who came before. No, he is different. My nemesis. This will be a good end.

The smell of coffee fills the air, soothing and comforting. Riding on the scent of the coffee is bacon and eggs and toast and home and safety and hope and everything will be fine because it's morning and the nightmares of the past fled from the encroaching glorious rays of the sun. The world will never end, ridiculous to believe it ever would. Peace will come, the wars on television will fade to nothing and a grand and golden age will finally and forever reign. Henry breathes deeply, filling his chest with promise.

Diana's side of the bed is still warm, still smells of her skin and hair. He stands and opens the curtains and the sun explodes into the room. The white snow glints with a million angles, endless variations, a miracle of complexity. Henry smiles.

He finds Diana in the kitchen and she smiles at him, she glows. She hands him a cup of coffee. He's warm, apart from the sip, apart from the forced heat, apart from all the outside world. Everything will be fine now. He knows, he's sure.

"Morning," he says to his wife.

"Good morning. Don't you mean good morning?" Diana smiles again.

"Yes, it is." Henry sips his coffee.

Diana turns and concentrates on breakfast. Bacon sizzles and eggs are scrambled.

"Is Arthur downstairs?" Henry asks.

"Oh yes, big doings in the city he said."

Henry almost touches her, wraps his arms around her, just to make sure she's real, that it's all real. He watches her scramble the eggs, moving deftly, as anyone could given such a task. But all her movements mean something and are beautiful, poetic, like ballet where each subtle gesture is a volume of emotion.

"You're beautiful," Henry tells her.

"Oh, I'm sure. Just out of bed."

"No, you're really beautiful. It's more than looking, it's who you are."

"That's a very nice thing to say."

Henry watches her and sips his coffee. "You don't believe me?"

She looks up from the eggs and out the window at the vast winter scene of the suburban neighborhood covered in a pure blanket of snow. "No, not really. I know you believe it. You really believe I'm what you say I am."

"Beautiful," Henry repeats. The coffee tastes good, maybe better than good, maybe the best ever.

Diana turns to him, looks at him standing near the kitchen table, in his robe, holding his coffee. She still holds the whisk, eggs dripping on the floor. "Yes, but it's not that I am beautiful or that I'm not. If you look out this window you may think it's beautiful, but you may also think it's cold or depressing or simply snow covered houses. And that's you Henry and that's always been you since I've known you. You never see things for what they are, the reality of it. Your perception dictates reality. And sometimes your perception is not based in reality."

"More from your self-help guru?"

"Yes and no. It's more like you've read something or saw something and you knew it, but you just needed someone else to tell you. You've always been like this, seeing what you want, if it's true or not."

"I'm going to check on Arthur." He steps closer to Diana and kisses her. "And you are beautiful," he whispers in her ear. "And you're here."

Arthur is sitting at the far corner of the city.

"Good morning, Arthur," Henry announces, smiling.

Arthur looks up, quizzical at his father. "Morning."

"How's life in the big city this morning?"

Arthur does not answer, but turns his gaze to the labyrinth of buildings and streets. Henry walks around the perimeter. He sips his coffee, which steams in the shadow filled basement. He pauses here and there and sips.

"Why are there so many people in the streets?" Henry asks.

"Something's happening," Arthur responds.

"Hmm."

Henry continues to circle the metropolis, looking for familiar faces and not looking. A large portion of the populace has gathered in the section known as Central City. Amongst these people, but separate, a space between him and the rest is the hero principal. Henry points to him and tells his son, "I saw him yesterday."

Arthur looks up and then back down. "A version of him," he responds.

Henry pauses in his pacing and sips his coffee. "Yes, I guess so, a version of him."

"Because he's different in my city."

"Yes, I suppose he would be."

"Everyone is."

Henry sips again and looks over Gotham, where more people stand in the streets.

"Mrs. Grayson. Did she ever find her son?"

"No. But she's not worried about him anymore."

"Why?"

"Something more important is happening."

"Can you tell me?" Henry asks, smiling.

"I'm not sure."

Henry looks down at his son, still enthralled by his city, the facets and the aspects of the lives. "You didn't say 'that would be telling.' That's what you always tell me."

"Sometimes things happen on their own. Sometimes I don't know what will happen."

Henry watches Arthur watch his creation. "Breakfast is almost ready."

"Okay."

Henry kisses his son gently and walks back upstairs.

He pours another cup of coffee and Diana places the plates on the table. Arthur appears and the family sits and eats breakfast together. Arthur relates a comical story about a classmate losing bowel control, a bully he clarifies, when confronted by the teacher. Arthur also expresses a modicum of excitement about the upcoming holiday. Henry tells the tale of his favorite Christmas gift. Diana smiles and reassures both of them that this Christmas will be the best yet. Henry smiles and laughs without restraint. The warmth of coffee and family washes over him, enveloping him, holding him and all the pangs of the past and the bitter cold of the world fade away. Diana eventually clears the plates and adjourns with Arthur to the living room. Henry watches them for a moment, standing in the archway that leads from the kitchen to the living room. The ringing of the phone pulls his attention away from the scene.

"Hello," Henry answers.

"Hey, Henry, it's Hal."

"Hal. What can I do for you?"

"Listen, I have a situation-"

"Is it Barry?"

"No." There's a pause. "It's Lance. He's been arrested. It's a long story, too much to explain over the phone. Could you possibly meet me at the county holding cell?"

"Why?"

"Lance asked for you."

"What's this all about?"

"The police called me because Lance had my card in his wallet as the president of the union. He didn't have anything else. They called and said he refused to talk to anyone but you. He asked for you specifically. He's being difficult they say. I said I would bring you down there. I'm trying to keep this quiet, Lance being a teacher for so long and all. Will you meet me?"

"I suppose I ..."

"Thanks, Hank. As soon as you can. I'm heading there now."

Henry walks back to the living room. Diana and Arthur are sitting together on the couch. The room is warm and cozy. He looks outside at the snow and cold. Lance should be fine. There's no real reason to go. He'll be fine. The lost and confused man will be fine. Here is safe. Here is perfect.

"I have to go out," Henry announces quietly.

"Okay, dear." Diana turns and smiles at him.

"I might stop at the hospital on my way home."

"Do you want us to come?"

"No, you stay here," Henry says and smiles.

Episode 26: A Flash

The air is brisk and Henry breathes deeply. His senses are alive. He sees the angles of reflected light, subtle in the snow, the glorious sun and great and beautiful blue sky. The snow crunches under his feet, somewhere in the distance children laugh. The world is open. Diana never asked him where he was going or why he had to go. He drives to the county holding cell.

Hal Allen is standing outside on the steps, clouds of white emanate from his mouth.

"Hey, Hank."

"Morning, Hal."

"Sorry to call you out like this, but it's all I could think of. The union will provide a lawyer, but Lance wanted to talk to you first. The police said he was adamant. I'm trying to keep this from getting out of control. With what happened to Barry and now this, well it's bad press."

"No problem. How's Barry holding up?"

Allen pauses and stares at Henry. "You okay, Hank?"

"I'm fine, never better in fact."

"Hmm."

"So what is it I can do?"

Hal sighs and rubs his eyes. "Lance was arrested last night in some sting operation. The police say he's been buying drugs for some time now. They've had his dealer under surveillance for months, watching who was buying. Last night they arrested everyone. When Lance was arrested they found my card in his wallet and called me. They said Lance requested to talk to you before anyone else."

"Drugs?"

"Heroin."

"Jesus."

"I know. He had nothing else on him, other than my card as president of the teachers' union. No driver's license, no credit cards, nothing. Only my card and scraps of paper. Computations by what the police said."

"What should I do?"

"Talk to him, I suppose."

Henry nods. The men enter the building, the front of which is bathed in sunlight, like a great cement face turned to God. A lone officer is seated behind a large desk, pentagon in shape. He smiles as Hal and Henry approach. He greets them.

"We're here to see Oliver Lance," Allen tells him.

"Yes, let's see. You're the union officials, right?"

"Yes."

The officer consults his computer. There's music playing in the background, Christmas music, *White Christmas* by Bing Crosby. There are decorations on the walls.

"Oh, there seems to be a mistake," the officer says as he looks up.

"What is it?" Allen asks.

"Lance was transferred late last night. Apparently there was an incident."

"Transferred?" Henry asks.

"Psych Center."

Henry recedes slightly, shying away from the other two men.

"Can we still see him?" Allen asks.

"Probably, I don't see why not. Just tell them over there that you were requested by the suspect before he was committed," the officer informs them with a smile.

"Committed," Henry repeats the word.

"They should at least let you know if he's okay." The officer smiles again.

Allen looks at Henry, then back at the young officer, still smiling behind his desk, his blue eyes almost reflecting the sunlight. Allen turns and Henry follows him into the glorious outside world.

The officer calls out, "Merry Christmas."

The two men pause on the steps. The sun is still shining brightly on the face of the building. "What do you think?" Allen asks.

"We should go see him," Henry answers.

Allen sighs again. "Do you know where the Psych Center is?"

Henry pauses and looks into the blue sky. "Yes."

"I'll follow you, then."

The two men walk down the steps shielding their eyes. The rest of the world is elsewhere, warm, happy and safe.

The County Psychiatric Center held the national record as the longest building in the world in 1901. Since that time a modern facility was built on the grounds, but the skeleton of the original structure still stands, now black against the blue sky. It's a landmark. The most striking aspect of the building are two towers that occupy the middle of the structure, two old appendages stretching to the sky. There was talk of renovating the space, making it into something, but no one cared enough to push the idea and the long building with the two towers remains desolate, holding onto the ghosts of past torments.

The sun remains dominant in the sky as Henry walks to the main entrance. The second building was constructed in the early 1970's and retains all the earmarks of that time's architecture. Allen follows behind, just off Henry's right shoulder. The reception area smells of disinfectant and urine. Henry approaches the receptionist to background music, Nat King Cole's *Hark the Herald Angels Sing.*

"We're here to see Oliver Lance," Henry announces, his voice echoes slightly. He and Allen are the only two in the reception area.

"Sorry, visiting hours don't start until noon." The receptionist does not look up. She's losing her hair, angry that she has to work, angry at the time she has left.

"He asked for us before he came here." Henry's voice is a whisper now, as if he's afraid.

"Are you his lawyers?" He left her because she wasn't attractive anymore, her weight and the years, her work, it all took so much from her.

"No…"

Allen moves forward, taking charge, reluctant, but knowing the answers, always knowing the answer. "We are his representation from the union."

The receptionist finally looks up, her glasses have slid to the tip of her nose, her name is obscured by a variety of holiday stickers. "So, are you his lawyers or not?"

"We are," Allen answers.

"Have a seat and the doctor will be with you in a minute." She picks up the phone and talks into the receiver. Her movements have an exhaustion about them, like the next one might be the last, but she won't let it.

Henry and Allen sit in molded plastic chairs. The television is on and voices filter above them quietly. Henry gazes at the room. A slight film seems to cling to the walls and ceiling. Quick glimpses of madness and absolute loss graze on his power. But Henry looks beyond those phantoms, past the gray film of decay and out the lone window to the white and open world; hope and endless hope. A door opens and a man in the proper lab coat and thick glasses appears.

The doctor clears his throat. "You must be Mr. Lance's representatives."

Henry and Hal stand. All three men shake hands, while Frank Sinatra plays in the background. "We are," Hal says. "We're actually from the teacher's union. I don't want there to be any confusion."

The doctor looks at them over his glasses, examining them. Henry winces quickly, blocking his power that grows ever more demanding. "I don't suppose it actually matters," the doctor says quietly. "Do you know of any family?"

Hal looks at Henry. "Hank?"

"I don't think he has any left. His wife is gone," Henry responds.

"You're Henry Kent?" The doctor moves closer as he asks the question, seemingly interested.

"Yes."

The doctor's eyes narrow, looking into Henry. "Do we know each other? Your name is familiar."

Henry attempts to resist the urge to unleash his power and delve into the doctor and the ghosts that haunt the reception area. "No," he whispers.

The doctor brings his hand to his mouth as if he is going to ask another question, but does not. He simply nods his head and changes the subject. "He's been asking for you, talking about you. Would you like to see him?"

Henry pauses, he can't feel the sun and the snow anymore or the cold of the air, it's all blocked out now, all of it just beyond the thick door. "I suppose I should."

"Follow me then." The doctor turns and Henry looks at Hal.

"I'll wait here," Hal whispers.

Henry nods. The doctor resumes his pace and pushes back through the door he came from. Henry watches Allen take his seat again and stare up at the television. He then follows the doctor through the familiar white door. Henry enters a long corridor with several doors lining each side. As he follows the doctor, he glances through several windows to find each door hides a little sitting area, almost cozy. A couch, a chair, even plants make each individual room welcoming.

Episode 26, Part 2: A Second Flash

"This is different from how I… pictured the asylum," Henry mutters.

"It's somewhat new. Most of our patients are self-committed. They just need to talk."

"Hmm."

"However, Mr. Lance being brought in by the police, was placed in a more secure area."

Henry continues to trail the doctor, turning right and left, up a flight of stairs and eventually stopping before an armed guard sitting at a desk.

"Good Morning, Ronald," the doctor greets the guard.

The guard looks up from a magazine. His small radio plays orchestral Christmas music, something from the Nutcracker, Henry imagines. "Good morning, Dr. Raymond," he says with a grin.

"How is everything this morning? No trouble I hope."

"No, everything is quiet. All the patients got their meds and it's been dead since."

"Good, good. Would you buzz me in? This gentleman is here to see Mr. Lance."

"Oh." The guard looks Henry over, trepidation, fear, happy to stay away. Henry closes his eyes quickly. This place is too emotional, too determined to be known. There is a buzz and Dr. Raymond passes through the doorway. Henry pauses again, but follows.

They enter a new corridor, darker than the other one. The lights are dulled, subdued and shadows dwell in all the corners. "This is our high security wing," Dr. Raymond explains. "These patients require more supervision and thus are kept here, where they can be better helped. Most of these patients aren't really dangerous, but must be isolated in order to provide them with a better chance to get well. It's only rarely that we have a criminal. There's a facility further out in the county that is better equipped to handle those types of disorders. Here we are." Dr. Raymond stops abruptly.

Henry stands before a great gray thick door, Lance's name is printed on a card to the right. He looks through the small window. Lance is sitting on a cot, rigid, looking at the wall.

"Is he all right?"

"He's in the process of detox. It seems he's a heroin addict, as well as several other narcotics, judging from his blood test. We found evidence of several hallucinogens, which might explain his behavior. But as I said he shouldn't pose any danger. And he should be happy to see you."

Dr. Raymond punches a code into the keypad on the door, which opens slowly, dramatically. Henry stands just at the threshold, looking in, looking at Lance.

"Go on now. I'll be right outside." Dr. Raymond closes the door, forcing Henry to step in.

He takes a moment to calm himself and shut down his power. He thinks of Diana. The room is a steel blue, quiet and still. There is a cot, a sink and a toilet. Lance remains seated, dressed in pajamas, his hands resting on his knees. Henry is warm, his overcoat weighing on him. He steps in front of Lance and leans against the opposite wall. He can feel the sweat on his back and craves to be outside in the cold.

"I knew you'd come." Lance's voice is quiet, but rich in Henry's ears, melodic and deep. There is a bruise on his right cheek.

"Yes?"

"I knew, as I know all sorts of truths." Lance's eyes are focused on Henry's chest. He does not look up.

"Oliver, what happened?"

"What was supposed to happen." His words glide on the air, hover as a breeze in summer.

149

"Drugs? Oliver? You're an addict?"

"Yes and no. I chose to take the drugs and I repeated that decision. I needed a gateway, time had made me stagnant. I couldn't think beyond myself. I knew it was there, out there, but beyond me somehow. The drugs made sense. History is ripe with stories, fictional or true, of drugs allowing insight. They were my bridge to understanding."

"Oliver?" Henry removes his coat and holds it before him, but not defensive, not afraid.

"The math, Henry. Listen, listen carefully. It's almost here, the end of it. I can feel it, really feel it. The math, Henry, the numbers all make sense, they all add up now and it's soon, it's so close, so very close." Lance's voice grows more resonant, but near the edges, there's a thinness, the richness fading slightly. "Now, Hank, I told you how to figure it out. Did you? Did you do the math?"

"Oliver…"

"Math." Lance's voice rises and echoes in the small room. "It comes down to the numbers. Numbers don't lie. They can't, they won't, not to me, not anymore."

Lost and alone, terribly alone, a wasteland of nothingness, no net, no safety, not even the job, not even a hobby, nothing and the world doesn't care. Henry closes his eyes quickly, forcing them shut.

"Numbers, numbers, numbers, numbers, numbers…"

Henry keeps his eyes closed, moisture at the corners.

"Hank, Hank, look at this." Lance stands and removes his pajamas and is naked, but covered completely, from neck to ankle in tattoos: numbers and equations, squares and circles, diagrams and symbols. He turns and his back also bears the marks, symbols, pi, multiply and divide, addition and subtraction. He is an equation, he is his dementia.

"Look at this." He points to his chest. "This is the one, this is the one that brought it all together."

"What is it?" Henry tries to step back, but the wall stops him.

150

Lance comes closer. Henry can smell it, hanging on the man like chains, weighing him down, invisible, but now known, evident in the bright room: despair, utter and total, not genius, not the mad truth speaker, knower of secrets, but a shell, empty and wanting, the smell of decay in its most perfect form. Lance's voice is a whisper when he says, "It's the formula for happiness."

"What?"

Lance explains what the 'A' means and why it's divided by the 'B' squared, because 'B' is important. Then there's the 'C' and the 'D' and the 'E', which is multiplied by the 'F', but the 'F' is the sum total of the 'H' and the 'G', and somewhere the age of the subject must be factored in. Lance's smile does not diminish as he explains the process.

"Did you come up with this?" Henry moves his coat, his shield, protecting himself knowingly.

"No, no, no." Lance moves away, towards the toilet. "I read it. A book I bought, self-help, by the wife of the hero principal. I knew him. We talked before he was shot. I know her too. And I read her book and it was there, the math and maybe that started it too, but no, I think it was always there and the book just showed me it, but it was here before, and the drugs opened the door, the book was the door and then I knew, and then I could do it, the formula and the starting point."

"But the tattoos?"

"It's too important. I needed it with me all the time, could never forget it if it's always there, and there it is. Even when the darkness comes closing in and it is so very close now. I'll know the secret and I'll be happy once I do the math, once I solve all the problems and then it'll be over."

"Oliver, it's…"

Lance looks at Henry suddenly, piercing through the coat and the shield. "You know, don't you? The truth of it, the grand and beautiful truth of it. The world will end and we can start over, fix our mistakes, and she won't leave, and it'll be better, it'll be perfect."

Henry hangs his head, tired suddenly, leaning against the wall, holding it up. Lance approaches him, smiling a broad grin.

"You know, don't you? You did the math."

Henry looks up. Lance's face is wrinkled and old. His hair is a mess. He seems out of place, lost in the small cell. Lance reaches out and touches Henry on the shoulder. Henry stares at his hand, yellow at the fingernails, age spots discoloring his skin.

"You know?"

Henry feels it, the welling of the emotion. "Get your hand off me." Henry swipes at it and Lance steps back, falling slightly. Henry pushes him farther away. "I believed you. I thought you knew and I even accepted it. But you don't know anything. You're just like my father, weak, pining for a woman, broken by a relationship that ended. You can't look after yourself without a woman. You're pathetic."

"Hank, don't..." Lance's eyes gaze down. He sits on the bed and pulls his legs to his chest, naked and alone.

"Drug addicted old fool."

Henry slams his hand against the door, which opens. Dr. Raymond steps into the cell and gives a cursory glance to Lance and then ushers Henry out of the room closing the door.

The corridor is quiet for a moment. Raymond is still holding on to the doorknob as an anchor to something solid when he asks, "Did he say something disturbing?"

Henry sniffles and wipes his eyes. "Nothing, nothing but ramblings." Henry dons his coat.

"Hmm."

"What will happen to him?" Henry asks.

"He'll be here for a few days. We'll evaluate him, he'll go through detox. And then, probably prison or a state facility."

"Then what?"

"I don't know."

The two men turn and walk slowly to the guarded door. Henry avoids eye contact with the doctor and looks at the doors with the corresponding names; people behind thick gray metal highlighted by a small window so they can be observed, watched and known. Henry thinks of the dimensions of the window in relation to the door, the percentage of light versus darkness. He wonders if the designer considered the idea of the whole door, if that mind considered that the window made the door darker by comparison and made the world darker by comparison. The names are hand written, transient, the people unable to stay, forced to move on and the printed name is cast away.

Then a name catches Henry's attention and he comes to an abrupt halt. Raymond doesn't notice and continues on, walking close to the opposite wall, almost leaning against it. Henry remains rigid, but then slowly, with great apprehension shuffles to the name and the door and the window.

Through the window he sees a woman sitting on her cot, her arms folded as if she might be holding a child. Her face is serene, her white skin reflects the lights and her eyes seem as pieces of coal, dark and infinite. Her hair falls over her face and drops on her shoulders. She seems a slight woman, fragile in her pajamas. Henry notices abrasions on her wrists, pink on her skin. Her head begins to turn slowly. Henry wants to look away, pull a shade or stop her. But there she is, looking at him, her eyes sparkling, a brilliant light in the vastness of dark. Life and no life at all, everything and nothing. Her mouth, thin and delicate begins to coil at the corners and Henry knows she's not there, not here, but between and above and below, untouchable, nothing of reality or belief, beyond it all now, beyond history, right and wrong, beyond all that is life, all that is humanity. Her face beams to him and through him, his power unable to compensate. The light engulfs the room, and pushes through the window and burns the door and burns the room and the world with it.

"Mr. Kent." Dr. Raymond's hand is on Henry's arm. "Mr. Kent, please, this is not permitted."

"What?"

"You can't just stare into any room you want."

"Oh."

Dr. Raymond moves Henry from the window and leads him down the corridor.

"I thought I knew her," Henry whispers. "Her name…"

"Grayson?"

"Yes. I thought I knew her name."

"Do you?"

"Yes."

They pass by the security guard, who smiles as Judy Garland sings *Santa Claus is Coming to Town.*

"Why is she in the secure area?" Henry asks.

"I'm afraid that's confidential." Dr. Raymond grasps the arm rail and leans heavily on it.

"I don't suppose it matters. She's there and that's what's important in the end."

"What's that?"

"Nothing."

Dr. Raymond stops at the white doors that separate the interior of the asylum from the waiting area. He looks Henry over one last time. He takes Henry's hand and shakes it and wishes him a Merry Christmas. He then walks away back into the asylum.

Allen is seated alone in the waiting area. The glorious sunlight, beacon of hope, has faded slightly, a gray about the edges, real suddenly and capable of dying or simply fading away.

"How did it go? How is he?" Allen asks.

"I'm not sure. Horrible, I suppose."

Allen looks at the television. "Terrible thing."

"You know, I should have known something was wrong," Henry tells him.

"C'mon now. The guy was always a little different."

"He told me the world was coming to an end."

Allen looks again at the television. "He might be right."

"What?"

"It's all over the news. Rogue nation in the Middle East has tested a nuclear device."

"Jesus."

"I guess there has to be some response."

"War?"

"World War III."

Henry looks out the window. Allen continues to stare at the television. "Look, Hal," Henry begins. "I have to get home. If there's any more I can do, let me know."

"That's fine, Hank. I appreciate you coming."

The men shake hands. Henry walks to the door, pausing to look back over his shoulder. Allen is seated again, entranced by the television. The receptionist has appeared and stands behind him, staring up at the pictures that flash and listening to words of apprehension. Henry opens the door and walks into the lessening sun and the growing gloom.

Episode 27: Colored Lanterns

The radio is dominated by the breaking news of the nuclear threat. Henry listens, his focus waxing and waning. As he stops at a signal, Carter crosses the street and smiles at him. Henry smiles back. The car moves again and Carter's voice announces that the nations of the west are discussing a response to the growing international crisis. For the remainder of the drive Carter tells him about the world and how it has changed in the last hour.

Henry finds Diana and Arthur at the kitchen table. Both smile and greet him. The smell of bacon lingers in the air. As Henry sits and begins to ask them important questions, the phone rings.

"Hello."

"Hello, Henry."

"Good morning, Mom."

"I have some sad news."

The sun fades further behind the growing gray clouds. "Dad?"

"I'm afraid he's passed away."

"He's dead?"

"Yes."

Henry breathes quickly and looks at his wife and son. "When?"

"This morning. Suddenly. Quickly."

"Hmm."

"Could you come up to the hospital? I need your help." She adds, "It shouldn't take too long."

"Yes."

Henry takes a moment to explain life and death to his son and kiss his wife good-bye. Her lips taste empty and her eyes are far away. The television is on in the background.

The radio is enraged by the thought of nuclear Armageddon. Scenarios of the day after, the aftermath of a nightmare are discussed in terms of casualties and survivors. Carter speaks of the audacity of a people to threaten all people over simple differences. He frets as to what might happen to life on the planet because of the emotions of a few. He tells the world to use duct tape for protection against radiation. A caller asks Carter how this rogue nation was able to produce a nuclear weapon. Carter tells the caller that's not important, it only matters that they have it and that they intend to use it and that they want to die and that they want to kill. He tells Henry about bomb shelters and how to prepare for the end of the world.

As Henry pulls into the parking ramp of the hospital Carter hands him a parking ticket. Carter greets him in the lobby and then again in the elevator.

His mother greets him in his father's room, his father is still in the bed, and looks much as he did when he was alive. Henry hugs his mother tightly, rests his head on her shoulder and holds back his tears.

"Oh, my dear, it's all right," his mother tells him as she holds him. "It's going to be fine."

Henry continues to hold his mother as a child would. He remembers when she held him when he was young and the world was too cruel for him. She would hold him for hours. He wouldn't cry, would never cry. He imagined her taking his tears as her own so he wouldn't have to feel the pain. Eventually they would separate. She steps back from him now and he is left to stand on his own. He looks to his father, his eyes are closed, seemingly peaceful. Henry approaches the bed. His father's skin seems thin, like paper, and the slightest touch would reduce him to dust.

"He looks... old," Henry whispers.

"Yes. At the end he aged quickly."

"He doesn't look like him."

"Don't remember him this way. Remember him as you like."

"Hmm." Henry leans over the body. He notices marks left by the IV, minor abrasions on the arms, marks on his body, possibly the last thing he felt. Henry thinks of his father as a young man with a young wife and a young child. He remembers his father's hands were strong, powerful, able to hold the whole world. "Diana told me that I don't see things for what they are. She says I see them as I would like them to be."

His mother steps to the opposite side of the bed. "We all do."

"Maybe."

"It will be all right, Hank."

"It shouldn't be like this. It should be black and white."

His mother smiles at him, a reminiscent smile, a smile Henry remembers. "You were always worried about that. It's like when you would go on your walks. I thought you were running away, but your father said it was just something you had to do. We never called the police. You would eventually just come back."

"Hmm."

Henry watches his father in silence for a time. The sun fades further away amongst the gray clouds.

"What do we do now?" Henry asks.

"I'll take care of everything."

"I thought you said you needed me."

"I wanted you to see him, one last time. I'll take care of all the arrangements."

"Is that why you came back?"

"It would seem so."

"Hmm."

They stand together, but apart, separated by Henry's father. Eventually Carter comes in to remove the body, he nods to Henry and offers his condolences. Henry is left with his mother in the otherwise lifeless room.

"Is there anything else I can do?" Henry asks.

"No. I'll take care of everything. Go home and we'll talk later."

They embrace again, less forceful. She looks at Henry intently. She smiles and he smiles. "Go home," she tells him. Henry kisses her and departs.

He stands outside the hospital watching the clouds move across the sky. People walk past him and offer greetings, bundled as they are, holding tightly to their coats and scarves. Henry would tell them that his dad is dead.

"He wasn't a great man, maybe not even a good man, but he was my dad and now he's gone. I don't want a monument to him or a holiday in his honor or even a local news story. I just want someone other than me to acknowledge he's dead and that he was alive. I know it's selfish to want the world to stop, but I do. And it's more than that. It's more than him dying. And it's crumbling around me.

Carter smiles at him and wishes him a Merry Christmas.

"I know it's futile to think this was important. Useless and childish. People will remember him, friends, coworkers, they'll remember the good and the bad. They'll tell stories and anecdotes, tie certain things to memories of him. But for just a second there should be a pause and the world should know my dad is dead."

Carter bumps into him. "Sorry, buddy. My wife's having a baby." Carter is near giddy, placing both hands on Henry's shoulders.

"My dad is dead."

"What? Merry Christmas, pal." Carter runs away.

"It won't matter anyway. Nothing will come of this."

Henry clenches against the cold and walks to his car.

The radio is again alive with panic and the impending doom of the world. Already there have been reports of religious zealots claiming to have known it would come to this. Already stories of suicide and hysteria have begun to filter in. Already people have begun to back away from the world, isolation and safety. Carter tells the listeners all this and more, the beginning of the end. Henry listens and drives home.

Episode 28: Creatures of the Night

Hands are shaking again. Can't stop it. Dropped the hammer and the saw after that. He's passed out. Sit down for a minute. Can't show my weakness. This is right. This is right. This is right. Wake him up. Make him watch me light the welding torch.

You see it all fades in the end. All the accomplishments and more than that, all the philosophies that society is built on, all those noble rules and perfect examples, all that fades and will be pushed aside. When the end comes all the beauty, all the discoveries, all the genius efforts over the years will be dust. They won't even be a memory. No religion, no hope can stand against that. Isn't that terrible? Isn't that ultimately the horror of the world? Consider Pythagoras, the man who came up with the very basic principle of Math, so perfect in its simplicity. When the world ends, he dies again and for all time. His genius will mean nothing in the great fire that will engulf the Earth.

There is a muffled whimper. The blue flame reflects off his open eye, he has blue eyes.

You think I'm being melodramatic. You think that I'm making something better or greater than it is. Pythagoras and Newton and Einstein and all the great mathematicians and their grand work will be as if they never even existed, never mattered, never were the basis of life. This is fact. This will happen. Now or years from now, what does time matter? We have only our conscience to serve. The greater good as we see it, is the only thing of real importance. Because we're all ash in the end.

The tape has fallen from his mouth and his screams are so loud.

The kitchen is empty. The plates are clean and are in the sink. The house is quiet, no television, no radio, no sound other than the constant hum of the furnace. Henry gazes out the kitchen window. The sky has turned a light gray, the sun is still there above the clouds, but the night is beginning to encroach at the edges, and will, given time, engulf the sky. Long shadows cross the house. One light, in the kitchen provides the only respite from the ever-growing shadows.

"Hello," Henry says quietly.

His voice is lost in the house, like he isn't even there. He moves his arm, unsure if he moves at all, if he disturbs the air around him. He thinks of his father, lying in the morgue, cold perhaps, in a metal drawer, waiting for what will happen next.

"Hello."

He thinks of Carter, walking from room to room, dripping here and there. Maybe he paused to allow a pool of blood to form, watching it grow on the floor or on the counter. Perhaps, out of some learned behavior or punishment, he avoided the carpet or furniture, afraid to stain it, a memory, a mark of who he was.

"Hello."

Henry leans on the table, suddenly overcome by his power. The earth, the people about him, all of them, fear and anxiety and worry, out of control, beyond control and it's getting worse, rushing to the end.

"Hello."

"Down here, Dad." Arthur's voice wafts up from the basement.

Henry finds his son sitting at the far corner of the city, the border between Gotham and Central City. The child sits back watching. From time to time he moves a person into the streets.

"Where's your mother?"

"In the street, like everyone else."

"Your real mother, Arthur." Henry's voice is louder than he intended.

"Real?"

"Arthur."

Arthur sighs. "She left."

Henry shudders. "Where did she go?" His voice is softer.

"I'm not sure." Arthur moves a person from a building to the street.

"Will she be back?"

"I'm not sure." Arthur sits back and watches.

"Did she say anything?"

"I'm not sure. Not that I remember."

"Arthur," Henry shouts. His voice echoes. His body has moved forward, beyond his control, bumping the table, causing several people fall.

Arthur looks at his father and sighs again. He stands and replaces the fallen people.

"Sorry, I'm sorry." Henry steps back and sits on a stool. "She'll be back. She said she wouldn't leave, she said she'd take me with her."

Henry looks at the city. Thousands of pictures stand in the streets, all facing the center, all looking as one, all feeling as one. His power at work on the pictures, on versions of people.

"What's happening?"

Arthur scans the city, standing and looking over the buildings and the people. He moves quietly amongst the canyons of Gotham and Central City, touching things, moving things, placing them where they should be. His grand plan coming to life before him, but growing beyond him, his creation taking a life of its own, forgetting the god that made it, that cared about it for a time. The god has also grown and moved beyond the city, moved to something new. "I'm not sure anymore. It seems it's gotten away from me. All the people are moving on their own."

Henry watches Arthur as he ducks here and leans back there, focuses on one person in the throng and then the throng in general. Arthur's voice has been quiet, ghostlike in the basement, there and not there, real and not real. Henry asks, "Arthur, are you all right?"

The boy sits down again, his eyes still on the city and the hidden corners of the world, where lives are lived and lost, unknown and meaningless. "I think so."

"You would tell me if you knew, wouldn't you? If you knew if something was wrong?"

Arthur looks at his father, his face suddenly apparent in the dim light. "I would, Dad. I would tell you."

Henry sits on the edge of the stool watching his son move more people into the street. He looks for Diana, but she is lost in the crowd. The only recognizable face remains the hero principal, standing apart and alone. "She left," Henry whispers. "She just left."

Time passes and Arthur asks about dinner. Henry is stirred from his search of faces and trudges upstairs to order a pizza. When the food arrives he calls to Arthur who emerges and takes his place at the table.

"This is Sunday," Arthur announces.

"Is it?"

"You know it is."

"Yes, I know."

"It's not pizza night. Things are different."

"It seemed easy."

"Oh." Arthur bites into his pizza and Henry follows. Arthur chews and drinks his soda. "Is Grandpa dead?" he asks.

Henry shivers, the cold he thinks. "Yes. Grandpa died today."

"Hmm."

"There'll be a funeral," Henry tells his son.

"I know."

"Are you sure your mother didn't say anything before she left?" Henry asks.

"She talked on the phone and then said she had to go."

"That's it?"

"Yes."

The night drags on and the temperature plummets to well below freezing. Arthur is put to bed and kisses his father good night. Henry lies on his side of the bed, waiting for Diana. He thinks of her as a doll again, a plaything to be twisted and posed based on his whims, something unreal to be held when all real things lose meaning and the only important things, the only beautiful things are the invented things.

Episode 29: The Wonder of it All

The skin bubbles a little before it goes black. Then it's like paper and flakes off and floats on the air. The smell is terrible, as bad as they say. It doesn't bleed much. I guess that's something.

The great crisis is not whether the hero is a hero but whether the hero can maintain his or her heroism over a prolonged period. The initial rush fades in time, fades to the smoldering embers of a childhood dream. It begins to seem far-fetched, because the world is changed through hard work and common people and not people dressed in gaudy costumes. The hero decides whether the examples of heroism are enough in a world that is too big for small adventures, a life saved here, a villain defeated there. Is it enough? The hero must ask this question. But most heroes do not live in a vacuum. Most heroes have a support system of other heroes, a universe designed for them to live and fight. But the realistic hero, that hero that lives with all the rules and limitations of reality must make this choice eventually. And this choice must be near impossible. With the reality of simple and ordinary problems: taxes, shopping, laundry, will the hero succumb or listen to the greater calling, if it is indeed a calling. The fact of the matter is a hero, a superhero could never exist in the real world. They're already a joke, heroism itself a punch line, relegated to a fringe community bent over comic books and hoping that movies might live up to their imagination, that actors can capture the radiance of the brightly clothed man or woman, fighting the grand fight with wonderful powers and weapons. The real world would never tolerate a break in the façade of decorum, such as the superhero. This is the truth, the ultimately sad truth of the world. The impossible is impossible. There will never be a Superman, because he would be rich and famous and never a modest reporter. The world will not tolerate those who wish to do good, those who are gifted and seek nothing more than to help. This is the world, the reality of it.

His head hangs limp. The smell is evident suddenly. The light is less dim suddenly. There is a realness to it suddenly. There were no tears at the end. No terrible scream. No repentance. Nothing earth shaking. A soft whimper, a gurgle, a final breath. Quiet, very quiet.

The morning is quiet. The sun is gone, hidden forever behind giant gray clouds. Arthur is also quiet, moving through the house, touching things that she touched, covering her fingerprints with his own, as if she never came back.

"You're going to be late for school. I have to drop you off early," Henry tells him.

"I don't have school today. Remember it's Christmas break. It's early because of the snow. I told you. Do you remember?"

She's still here, her ghost. Nothing is very different, but she was here, Henry is sure of that, the plates in the sink, the missing eggs, the bacon, a folded magazine, an indentation in the couch, the bathroom. Arthur prepares his own breakfast, cereal and milk, and some juice.

"Are you all right?" Henry asks.

"Yes, are you?" Arthur responds.

She came back and left again. There must have been something to make her leave, something that happened or will happen. Maybe she knows. She and Lance know, but that's not it. Lance is insane, drug addict, lost and confused. Arthur reads the back of his cereal box and Henry makes coffee.

"Yes, I'm fine. There's nothing wrong. Maybe I'll call in, can't leave you by yourself. Stupid anyway, going to school today. Tomorrow is the start of my Christmas break, dumb to make the kids come in for one more day."

"What's that?" Arthur asks.

"Nothing."

Arthur looks back to his cereal as milk drips from his chin.

"Maybe I should call Grandma, maybe she could watch you. But she might be busy." Funeral arrangements, "She's probably taking care of that. She knows what he would want." Doesn't she? They were married. "For a long time. They probably talked about it. I never told Diana."

"Dad, you're not making any sense."

Henry looks at Arthur, his face partially hidden by the cereal box. The coffee maker beeps. "What's that? Oh sorry. I didn't get much sleep last night. I guess I'm over tired."

"It's weird. I've never seen you do this before."

"What?"

"Talking like that."

Henry looks at his son. "Where did you get that cereal?"

"From the cupboard."

"You got it yourself?"

"Yes."

"When did you start doing that? I've always gotten breakfast for you. Today is Monday, isn't? Monday is muffins and jam."

"You seemed busy. So I got it myself."

"You've never done that before."

"Hmm."

Henry pours the coffee and watches it steam. He stirs in cream and sugar, and the color changes. "Maybe you could come to school with me. We're really not doing anything today."

"No. I have things to do today, in the basement."

"But your mother isn't here."

"I know."

"You can't stay by yourself."

Arthur pours another bowl of cereal and mixes in the milk. Henry watches his coffee and tries to remember getting dressed.

"I know. But she might come back. One of us should be here, even if she just calls," Arthur says as he crunches on a mouthful of cereal.

"You're right," he's right, "she might call and," she might not. She might be gone again and might not come back this time. "Gone again." Focus, so much to do and the world is ending, "and there's so much to do." Have to think, can't think. School, safe, clear. "I have to go to school." Call Mom. "I'll call your grandmother."

"You're doing it again, Dad."

"What?"

"Not making any sense."

"Oh."

Henry picks up the phone and dials the number. It rings twice before his mother answers.

"Hello."

"Mom, it's me, Henry."

"Good morning, dear. It's early."

"You're up," Henry responds.

"I guess you have a point. I didn't sleep much last night. I was thinking of your father."

"I know, I'm sorry. I have a problem."

"Oh?"

"It's Arthur. He doesn't have school today and Diana is … gone."

There is a sigh and some rustling on the other end. His mother's voice is soft when it returns. "You could call in, family emergency and all. Your father."

"I know, I know I should. But I want to go to school. I just want…" Henry pauses. "I want to get back to something I know, something concrete. Do you understand?" Work it out, find the solution, there's always a solution.

"I understand. It's what you do."

"What's that?"

"It's what you have to do."

"It'll be only today. Tomorrow there's no school. I could help you tomorrow with the arrangements."

"They'll wait."

"Don't you want to know about Diana?" Henry asks.

"Do you want to tell me?"

"Not yet. Can you be here in a half an hour?"

"Yes."

The line goes dead. As Henry turns, Arthur is suddenly before him. Henry jumps slightly. "You scared me."

Arthur sips his juice. "I'm sorry."

"Grandma is coming over to watch you. I have to get ready."

Henry moves about the bedroom, buttoning his shirt, finding a matching tie. The doorbell rings in time and Henry rushes past his mother and his son into the cold, bright world beyond the house. He is sure he told them goodbye.

The sky is clear, the beginnings of the sunrise appear on the horizon. The impending glory of the sun is known at the edges of the world and things seem limitless. But Henry feels it, softly, the knowledge the sky is finite, just beyond his vision, the end is near. His power moves beyond him and there is panic, dread, hope, and everything is everywhere at once. He pulls his coat closer, shuts it out and drives to work.

Several lights are on in the building, odd as he is just a few minutes later than normal. Henry trudges to school. The decorations that adorn the halls seem jovial beyond their intention, as if they actually mean something. Henry winces and with his head down he walks to his classroom, passing Carter, who smiles at him.

Attendance is sparse. Many students have stayed home and started the holiday early. Henry gives the students who are present a Christmas math puzzle and then allows them to talk of their upcoming freedom.

The day is compartmentalized, the class periods measured perfectly, the day broken up to fill the time exactly. Each student has a place, each moment has a purpose and nothing is left to chance or fate or anything random.

Henry watches their faces, bright and hopeful and there is no dread at Christmas. He avoids the faculty room, choosing instead to walk the halls in his free time, slowly and quietly, his footfalls echoing slightly. The halls are full of symbols of the season, colorful, childlike and innocent. He passes Lance's room and stops, mindless wanderings, no pattern and a destination.

The room is empty, no substitute, no children, nothing at all. He has not been in Lance's room in several years, not since Lance was assigned as Henry's mentor teacher. It's always been in the faculty room where they met. Lance would simply be there and Henry never had cause to seek him out.

He enters the room and waits for something to happen, ghosts, voices, a herald of something great and wonderful. But there is only the hum of the heater and the glass creaking against the winter breeze. The lights are on, but the room still seems dark, dreary and cold. Henry walks to the blackboard, a random name scribbled in nervous handwriting, the sub, most likely. The desks are in neat rows, uniform, five across and six deep, all of the same make and color.

Henry sits at Lance's desk, front and center of the room. It's an older model, faded wood, a planning calendar without blemish is the only distinguishing feature. He looks through the drawers, expecting and not expecting, several pens and pencils, a protractor, a compass, and a calculator. In the second the drawer down on the left-hand side, way in the back is a small agenda, the one given out to students every year. This one from two years ago. Henry flips through it and finds each page is full of writings and computations.

For the month of May there are lists of facts dealing with numbers. Some are innocuous, stars on the flag, countries in Asia, number of presidents, and so on. Others are of a darker bent: number of stab wounds left by Jack the Ripper, number of rapes on average for Tuesdays, number of people named Carter who die in a given hour. March is occupied with famous dates as they would appear as numbers: 1211941, 3141879, 12251642, 563, 10141066, and so. November has Lance counting random things: number of people named Kara, number of hairs on his comb, number of times he thinks about his wife. The other months are also complete with a theme. Henry closes the book and puts in back in the drawer. He turns to the blank computer screen and the image of Carter is behind him, but he does not turn around.

"It's been a long time since we've talked like this," Henry whispers to the screen.

Since you started taking those pills when you were a teenager.

"And when I stopped."

That was bad. I try not to think about that time.

"Then this is bad."

Maybe.

"Is this the end of the world?"

The world ends all the time and is remade all the time.

"Is that from a comic book?"

Yes, where else would I get something like that?

"I don't know. Maybe it was true."

It is true.

"Oh."

But then truth, and this where we always differed, is fluid. Remember how the same character appeared differently depending on the artist? Larger cape, bigger ears, the truth was never the same.

"It should have been. It should have been easy to know, measurements…"

Math?

"Yes."

Life isn't like that.

"No, life is exactly like that. No one draws life. It doesn't change every twelve issues. It doesn't get relaunched when it gets boring or the story gets too complex. It is as it is."

Kind of sad, I guess.

"Yes, it's very sad."

He was a drug addict.

"Yes."

I was a messed up teenager.

"Yes."

Your wife.

"Yes."

Your son.

"Yes."

You.

"Yes."

Henry turns around and there is only the name of the substitute teacher scrawled on the blackboard, Mr. West. Approximately fifty-seven people named West die in America every month. Henry stands as the bell rings and walks out into the hall.

Children smile at him and he returns their gestures with a small grin. Carter also smiles as he disappears around the corner. Henry falls into the stream of children, standing above them. He walks with one of his students back to his classroom, the girl goes to her desk and he to his.

He watches as they all enter and take their assigned seats, no waiver, all as it was and will ever be. When the bell rings again they quiet down, a few mumbles and a whisper here and there, but eventually they look to him, waiting for him to begin.

Henry stands and moves out from behind his desk. Carter passes by and smiles at him. He stands before his students, their eyes on him, some even have their pencils at the ready. He knows more about each child than he should. He knows the full history of each child up to this point in their lives. He knows the parents of that one are divorced, her mom was cheating and the child has trouble sleeping at night. This one has an IQ several points lower than the rest of the class; his mom was an alcoholic. That one is smarter than the rest, but suffers from diabetes and is on the transplant waiting list; her father died when she was three in a car accident. Others have attention deficit disorder and take a variety of medications in order to exhibit basic control over their tendencies. Some are from divorced parents, one's parents are a homosexual couple. A myriad of problems at this young age, a mountain of emotional issues to overcome before high school. But they're still precious, still important, still worth fighting for. Henry steps back behind his desk and informs the class that after they complete the worksheet they may talk quietly until the end of the period.

Episode 30: Looking to See What's Chasing

O'Brien calls with three minutes to go in the day and asks Henry if she could speak with him before he goes home. The secretaries wish him a Merry Christmas as he enters the office. He smiles back at them. In the background Nat King Cole sings of angels. On the secretaries' desks there are cookies, candy and other festive wares of the season. It seems warm in the office, inviting, family at work, imposing good feeling and camaraderie on an otherwise impersonal atmosphere.

The three secretaries smile as they speak to him, big wholesome grins. Each has a holiday sweater on, colorful, joyful, hopeful. He smiles without effort in return. The door to O'Brien's office is closed and seems to be the only part of the office devoid of decoration. It remains a simple brown rectangle. The gray blind is pulled over the window, giving no clue to the season.

"Is she here?" Henry asks Dinah. The oldest one, the one everyone comes to if there's a problem.

The cheerful woman with the wise eyes, knowledgeable of the world of the school, stops humming *Silent Night* and answers. "Yes. She's with a student. Did she call you down?"

"Yes."

Henry looks at Dinah's bright sweater, silver bells across her breasts.

She moves closer to Henry and she smells of cookies. "Is it about Mr. Lance? Pity that. There's been reporters calling the school all day."

"Oh." Henry's power soothes, nothing hidden in this woman, simply silver bells and genuine concern.

"It's such a shame. He was so close to retirement. First Mr. Jordan and now this. Seems you don't know anybody anymore."

"Hmm."

"I've known Mr. Lance for twenty-five years. You couldn't have seen this coming. Drugs and all."

"Twenty-five years?" Henry remembers twenty-five years ago when he was five.

"Yes," she whispers, growing introspective. "You just don't know. He was always so quiet, but very polite. I guess we all have secrets."

"I suppose." Henry looks down at the woman as she stares out over reindeer and snowflake cutouts, and pictures of Santa Claus. He glances at the other secretaries, as they remain seated, typing at their computers, the music still playing softly above their heads. Henry sees the office as pieces of the whole, desks, chairs, people, all making the picture. For some reason he thinks to ask Dinah a question, having never thought to ask it before, inspired by Rudolf and Dean Martin's *Let it Snow*. "Do you know what happened to his wife?"

Dinah reaches for her cup of tea, her bracelet jingles. "She died. I think it was cancer, six or seven years ago. He didn't make a big deal of it. He only told me because I was a friend of her sister. It was a sudden cancer, ate her up in months, so very sudden. Such a shame."

"Yes, it is a shame."

O'Brien's door opens and there, standing simply in the glow of red and green, surrounded by a jazz inspired rendition of *Sleigh Ride* is the embodiment of evil. The boy, wearing a sweater with a bright lion embroidered on it, looks back at O'Brien.

"I will. Merry Christmas, Ms. O'Brien."

Henry moves closer to the boy and steps in front of him. He looks up at Henry, his head cocked to one side. His eyes are bright blue. He pauses for a moment and then steps around the teacher and walks out of the office. Henry watches him and remembers the bathroom and the tape and the fear.

"Henry," O'Brien calls.

Henry turns and walks slowly into the office. His mind is still in the bathroom, still in the stall with the remains of duct tape. He sits without thinking.

"Sorry to call you in at the end of the day like this. It won't take long."

"Who was that student?"

"Who?"

"That boy, that boy who was in here just now."

"Oh, that's Phil, Phil Gardner. The kids call him Fox. I know his parents, his father actually, high school friends. They're getting a divorce and his father asked that I keep an eye on him."

"You know him?"

"Yes. His father thinks he's been acting differently. The divorce is nasty. Then his best friend had that accident. He feels alone. Poor kid."

"Hmm."

"What is it, Hank?"

"I think he was the one I saw picking on that other student in the bathroom, the Digby boy."

"Fox?"

"Yes. I told you. Remember I caught him in the bathroom."

"Not Fox."

"Yes, I'm sure of it."

"Maybe he was just fooling around. Digby said it was another boy who attacked him. He's been suspended and there will be charges filed. The situation is already taken care of."

"But, I'm sure it was him. I'm positive."

"Maybe it was something else. But as I said, it was another boy who attacked Digby."

"And that's it?"

"What else is there?"

"Nothing, I suppose." Gotten to her. She knows the parents, more maybe, deeper, an unspoken threat. Weak woman, motherly, won't accept the truth.

O'Brien shuffles some papers and then settles again. "Well, to the matter at hand. I talked to Allen this morning. He said you and he talked to Lance yesterday."

"We did." Evil flourishes when good men do nothing.

"What did he say? Did he say anything about the school?"

"About what?" Walked out with no threat of retribution, nothing to say you're wrong and this will not stand.

"Well, you know he regulated all the vending machines in the school and in the faculty rooms. Do you think he took any money from those accounts?"

"No."

"Are you sure?"

"As sure as I can be. I guess he could have." But there are worse crimes. There is weakness and there is chosen weakness.

O'Brien sits back and folds her hands. "I hate to ask you this, but could you look at his books and see if there are any inconsistencies?"

"Inconsistencies?"

"You know what I mean."

Henry's mind is once again in the bathroom, the pain and the anguish. "Yes, I suppose I do."

"Can't be too careful."

Henry sees the boy again, the victim and all victims. "Careful? It's past that, isn't it? We were careful and now we have to react again. React to Lance," react to Digby, react to the nuclear war. "Action and reaction." But what is that first action? That action is never truly understood. The starting point. Henry pauses and looks around the room, not sure if he said anything.

"Hank, are you all right? What are you talking about?"

Henry sits back, the bathroom and the weakness, an addict and the end of the world, Diana and Arthur, Mom and Dad, starting and ending points. "I'm sorry, O'Brien. It's just that... with all that's happened... my father died yesterday."

"Oh my God, Hank." O'Brien stands and walks around her desk. She sits next to him and touches his hand. "That's terrible. I shouldn't have asked you that about Lance. You should be at home with your family."

Contact and O'Brien is open. "I couldn't be with them. I had to come to work, to something I know. But it's starting to sink in. Isn't that strange? Right here. Does that make sense? Does any of it make sense?"

"Of course it does." She retracts her hand, afraid, scared of what might happen, a friendship, a misunderstanding, dreams of something more. Is she married? "I can relate entirely. As you know, my son, my boy has leukemia. He's been getting worse of late... and I can't stand to see him in so much pain. He's so small, so tiny and weak. It breaks my heart to see him like that, so I come to work, where it's safe."

"I'm sorry to hear that."

She sniffles and takes a tissue, the last one from the box on her desk. "I haven't told anyone about him getting worse. I don't want people coming in and trying to talk to me about it."

"Doesn't that help?"

She laughs slightly, wiping a tear from her eye.

"What is it?" Henry asks.

"I read this book recently, it's by the wife of that hero principal, a friend gave it to me. In it she talks about coping

179

and discussing sad events with other people. And it just struck me, that this, what we're doing, it's something that she claims happens all the time and is the only way to really deal with life-altering, tragic events. I just read about it last night."

"About what?"

"She says the only people that can really sympathize are those who are going through an equally tragic event. Even those who have gone through something similar have the aid of the hindsight. But someone actually experiencing tragedy is the only real person who can understand. That's funny, don't you think? I feel better that you might know what I'm going through." O'Brien forces a smile through her thin tears. "She comments on how the tragic events bring us closer together. She tells stories of shared happiness; a vacation, Christmas, something that makes us smile, joyful times. Those times fade away and in the end lose their luster. But the tragic events remain sharp, because we're supposed to have learned something from the pain. You remember when someone close dies, but his or her birthday is forgotten. There is a grave reflection associated with tragedy, that whatever happened was important because it made you pause and question things, question everything. She asks if humanity is based on misery or an attempt to avoid it."

"Happiness is the absence of misery," Henry whispers.

"Yes. Look at this destruction, look at this death, look at this pain, and remember and think how to avoid this in the future. She talks about when her husband was shot and how she was called strong and brave and how it made you really think about things. Later she laughed at those people, laughed at their shortsightedness. Tragedy is everywhere and the lessons are never really learned because each individual must learn those lessons for themselves. That's why those who are enduring suffering find comfort in other people experiencing the same thing."

"My wife read the same book."

O'Brien grips his hand and looks at her feet. "It's at times like this I don't want to be happy. I think that if I do smile, really smile or let myself be excited, my boy, my son will die. It's like my misery keeps him alive. Like I've made this deal, as long as I'm sad, as long as I'm angry and frustrated, God will let my boy live."

"Hmm."

O'Brien loosens her grip and moves back behind her desk, away from Henry. "It sounds stupid, I know. But it seems logical to me. It seems the price I have to pay to keep my son alive."

"Life is like that, I suppose. Making deals and believing they matter. Isn't that coping? Didn't she write all about coping in her book?"

"Preparation she called it. But if I prepare for my son's death, then it will happen. I'm not ready for that yet."

"Yes, it seems that's the first part of letting go."

"Are you talking about your father?"

"Yes."

O'Brien leans forward on her desk. Henry can smell her perfume; she's not that upset. "All this can wait until after the holidays. Go home, Hank. Go home to your family."

Epilogue to Chapter 30: How Long Can Anyone Run?

Henry has a passing notion to stop at Lance's house, just to see if there are remnants of his former life and the time before, just to see if his wife was real, that she breathed and spoke and loved him. Lance lives close to the school, part of the community, a neighbor. Henry turns the wheel involuntarily and weaves among the houses, large structures set back from the street. Henry knows Lance's home, where he lives and lived. There was a party, years ago, maybe just before his wife died, early in Henry's teaching career. The beginning of everything, Henry thinks. Diana was with him for the BBQ, the Christmas party, New Year's or whatever the reason for the gathering. He recalls the exterior of the house, painted white with gold trim, pillars in the front. His car pulls to the curb before the home.

The snow is piled about the front porch. The other houses have a clear path to the front door, people who took the time and effort to make strangers feel welcomed. But Lance's front porch is a solid block of snow, not even a footprint, not a hint of disruption of the pure white façade.

The windows are dark, no car in the driveway which disappears around the back of the house. It's an odd neighborhood for a teacher, expensive; his wife perhaps could afford to live here.

Lights begin to appear, colorful decorations spark along the street. Lance's house remains dark. The windows seem like obsidian, as if there were nothing beyond them, nothing but the far-reaching blackness, nothing beyond the white world. Henry tries to recall the interior, the life within the house. He can't seem to recollect pictures, curtains, the touch of a woman. He cannot remember Lance in detail, how he behaved, how he looked. Diana might have been pregnant at the time, they left the party early.

A sudden gust of wind lifts snow and twirls it in the front yard. In the distance there are children laughing. Henry opens the car door slowly, pushing it against the wind. He steps out, not stepping on purpose, but carried. He walks to the opposite curb and stands in front of Lance's house. He doesn't feel intimidated as he imagined, the house is not a monument or an ancient structure built in honor of a made up god. It's simply a house, simply his house.

Henry steps into the deep snow and pushes his foot down. He looks again at the street, dotted with more and more lights. The driveways are clear, the sidewalks are clear, but Lance's house is encased. Henry steps back and stands motionless near the curb.

"He hasn't been here is some time."

The wind blows sharply, polluted with snowflakes.

"I should have known that for some reason. I should have known that."

With added urgency, Henry pushes through the cold back to his car, which pulls away quickly and speeds down the street through the gathering snowfall.

Episode 31: The Moments Before

Henry sits in his driveway watching the snow swirl around his house. The whirling flakes are not really falling but twisting in the air, running about the house in patterns of random gusts and lulls, like a snow globe tossed and shook by a child just to see the small specks move. The house seems set in the scene, quaint and pretty, part of the picture, without real life.

As Henry steps from the car the reality of the world returns, the sharp cold and the wind stinging his face. He staggers back, unwilling to cope, not ready for it yet. He trudges through the snow to the front door. He sighs quietly before opening it and then falls in. He can hear the television. He creeps to the living room to find his mother sitting patiently watching the news. The images flash through the room, thousands of random people, angry and scared, happy and cautious, the emotions of the world through the small screen. He watches people cry and scream, protest and die, and they seem flat, lifeless, turn the channel and they cease to be. He shuts his eyes tightly.

When he opens them again, Henry scans the living room. His mother is still unaware of his presence as she is transfixed by the television. Henry looks for signs of a woman's touch, proof that Diana lives and loves him. He knows she sat there, lied there with her hand balanced on her chin as if it were something delicate and might break. She kissed him by the window, next to the Christmas tree, she loved him on the floor in a moment of childish passion. But the memories are not real as they cannot live beyond him, cannot exist in the world by themselves.

"Hello, Mother," Henry whispers.

"Oh, hello, dear. I didn't hear you come in. I was so focused on this." She nods toward the television and the images it presents.

"Hmm."

"It's terrible."

"Hmm."

"Are you all right, Henry?"

"I'm fine, I think."

"So much is happening to us and to the world. I sometimes think this is the last day before something else changes. The last day I knew your father, the last day he was alive, the last words he said."

"The last day of the world."

She pauses and looks at her son, older now but still young, ghosts of the boy she knew, smart and aloof and pensive.

"Where's Arthur?"

"He's in the basement. His city, you know." She smiles at him, smiles at the boy who needed to be smiled at.

Despite his dread, unexamined until now, unacknowledged until now, he smiles back. He turns to the kitchen and the stairs that descend to the basement.

Arthur is sitting near Gotham, away from the tall spires of the city, away from the mass gathering of all the people. The orange glow of the space heater casts Arthur's long shadow on the wall and casts deeper shadows over the city, making great angles on the buildings, wild patterns, like a grand and glorious sunset of the world. Henry walks the perimeter of the city, taking a moment to look here and there, looking at faces, recognizing and not recognizing. The hero principal is evident, as he's been placed in the street, the circle of open space about him remains. Most of the citizens have moved to the center of the metropolis and stand in the street, facing a common center.

"Hello, Dad."

"Hello, Arthur. How was your day?"

"Fine. I went with Grandma."

"Yes? Where did you go?" Henry continues to circle the city. His father is in the street, his mother is not with him.

"The funeral parlor. She talked with a man who did not smile."

"She took you there?" Henry pauses near a picture of Barry Jordan surrounded by many people, among friends it seems.

"I wanted to go with her. She explained it to me. She said if I wanted to know what was going on, she'd tell me. She said I was smart enough to understand. She said I'm like you when you were my age."

Henry resumes his pacing. "She said all that?"

"Yes."

"What else did you learn?" Hal Allen is on a side street, turned slightly away as if he's looking at something else.

"She talked about Grandpa."

"Did she?" Near what's known as Coast City, several people stand near the beach, among them is a picture that nearly resembles Dr. Raymond.

"She said she was sad, but she thought it was going to be okay. I asked her why she thought that and she said thinking that it wasn't going to be okay was her only other choice and she didn't like that. I liked it when she said that."

"Hmm."

"We saw Grandpa in his casket."

Henry stops abruptly near Central City and looks up from a picture of O'Brien. "You saw his body?"

"It's okay, Dad. I wasn't scared. He looked the same as he did in the hospital. Not really different at all. Grandma said after Christmas there'll be a wake and people will come to say goodbye to him."

"Hmm."

"She said that's the best thing, to say goodbye."

"Is it?" Henry is finally standing next to his son.

"Dad?"

"Yes."

"Did you move some of the people?"

"What?"

Arthur looks down at the city. "People are moved."

"How can you be sure?"

"I know. I just know. It's not a lot of them, just some here and there." Arthur points to a familiar young boy and then another child. "Even you've been moved. That's how I know."

"Hmm."

Arthur looks over his city, his people. His eyes glance over those persons who have been moved across town, to Gotham without his aid or presence. The space heater continues to hum behind him. "So did you move any of them?"

Henry smiles at his son. "I don't think so."

Arthur looks up at his father, the underside of his chin, slight stubble, subtle changes in his appearance, alterations in who he is. "Hmm."

Henry begins to pace again, leaning over the tables, looking into the heart of the city.

"Where's your mother?"

Arthur watches him, studies him. "I told you I don't know."

"No." Henry gestures to the city. "Here."

Arthur cocks his head to one side. "That's the thing. I think she's been moved. I can't find her."

"Hmm."

Henry continues to pace, sticking his head in different parts of the city: the theater district, the financial district, the museums, history and fine arts. Lance is near the library, a pretty woman stands next to him. A police officer with a broad grin is near the expressway that leads out of the city. Behind him is a nurse, an older woman with glasses.

"Whatever happened to Mrs. Grayson?" Henry asks.

"Not much."

Henry pauses and looks at Arthur. "What do you mean?"

"Not much happened to her. She just sort of blended into the city. I think she's still looking for her son. Yes, she still is. But she, herself I mean, is part of the whole story."

"I'm not sure I understand."

"I think Grandma told me something like that and it made sense to me."

"Is she going to find her son?"

"I'm not sure she is. I'm not sure it matters."

Henry's voice gets louder. "It matters."

"To her, I suppose. But to the city, to the city itself, it doesn't."

Henry feels warm. He feels the apprehension of the city around him, the uncertainty of Mrs. Grayson. "Where is she?"

Arthur looks down at the tables, the milk cartons and the boxes, the faces and the pictures, the vast cityscape that has been built and nurtured for years. His eyes pass over Gotham, Coast City, Central City, the poor slums, the rich affluent section, the entire metropolis and then he sits back. "I don't know."

Henry's face goes red, overcome suddenly, the frustration of the city seeping into him. "Sometimes, that's not good enough." He turns abruptly, knocking down a building, which crashes into several people and they fall down. He looks at them and sees his father laying there, an older picture when he was young. "Sorry." He walks away from Arthur and walks upstairs, taking two at a time.

Episode 32: The Eyes of the World Close

Henry reenters the kitchen. A soft light creeps through the window giving the room a thin gray quality, the colors are lifeless, the counter, the sink, the floor. Henry opens the refrigerator and even that light appears dull. He rummages through the containers, pulling out orange juice. He pours a glass and as he's about to replace the container he notices something, grape juice, Diana's grape juice. Diana never liked orange juice. She always had to have her special grape juice.

"She was here."

Henry places the orange juice next to the grape juice.

"And she'll be back."

He takes his beverage into the living room and sits in the chair opposite his mother. The television shows scenes from around the world: Carter in London, Carter in Mexico, Carter the President of the United States.

"How's Arthur?" his mother asks.

"He's fine."

His mother shifts on the couch, almost deftly, to face Henry. "He wanted to come."

"And you talked to him, like you used to talk to me?"

"He wanted to know. He reminded me of you."

"He said that you said that."

"It's true." She smiles at him and sips her tea. "And how are you, Henry? How was your day?"

"Fine. Last day."

"Yes. Christmas Eve is tomorrow."

"Yes."

There is a pause and the television fills the void. Carter is claiming that his organization has a weapon capable of inflicting terrible pain and damage. He is determined that the world will know him and his wants. He's been raised in violence and now seeks to end his agony in one final act of sweeping rage.

"I heard there was an incident at your school," his mother says.

"Hmm?"

"A boy was attacked in the bathroom. It was on the news."

"Yes, but that's been taken care of."

The silence returns. A religious leader appears on the screen pleading for patience and peace. Another man of god then takes over, claiming that God's judgment has come.

"It's very cold today," his mother says.

"Yes."

"A white Christmas?"

"Yes."

Carter the announcer is asking questions of several men who claim different revelations based on the immediate threat of global Armageddon.

"What is it, Henry? What do you want to talk about?"

"I'm not sure, Mom. I'm not sure about much."

"Because of your father?"

"Yes, I guess that's what happens when someone's parent dies. You feel… adrift. I mean Dad was always there. He was always part of my day, part of my life."

"He still is."

"I suppose, but not in the real sense. He's dead and that's that."

"But we can hold on to what we know of him, what we remember, because all else fades in time."

"Where did you hear that?"

"I read it recently. I found a book in the kitchen and read some of it this afternoon. I think it's by the wife of that hero principal. I liked it."

"Diana was reading it."

"The author discusses letting go and the need to hang on."

"I don't like that phrase: hang on. It seems so basic, like there's nothing else to do. We simply cling to things. There must be more."

"It's true, though. Look at those people." She nods to the television, Carter the priest, Carter the rabbi, Carter the iman. "So willing to believe in something greater than ourselves, but aren't we the height of evolution? Yet there's the notion of faith and God and something above us. This is from the book: when it's boiled down, it's a fear of being alone in the universe. But we are alone, alone and together at the same time. Society, family and all the other connections to fight off the loneliness of the world, hoping through others we attain meaning and love and peace and joy. But it's those others that let us down in the end. Because they're human like us, with all our uncertainties and inconsistencies and history and baggage. We're ultimately faulty things, people are defective and imperfect animals. That's the great beauty and tragedy of humanity. The weakness that brings us together will, in the end, be our downfall."

"That's rather deep, Mom."

"We used to talk deeply when you were young. Remember? You were always interested in everything. Always very busy."

"Yes, I remember."

"Always looking for connections. Asking what this means and what that means."

"The answer, always the answer and the meaning."
Henry gazes at the television, men are speaking of meaning,
what this means, what that means, what it will mean in the end.

"Meaning," his mother says to the room. "We force
meaning. That always annoyed you. You would get so
frustrated. But that was also your great talent, your most
profound talent. You could make anyone into something grand,
make them mean more than they actually did. You could give
them depth and meaning and wondrous aspects that in reality
they never possessed. But you saw it, saw it all, all that they
were and all that they would be." She smiles a great and
angelic smile, a smile of all smiles. "We were all part of your
story, Henry, and we were all more than we are in real life and
that's why we loved you."

Henry watches his mother watching him, a look of all
mothers on her face, with all the meaning of that relationship.
Henry looks down at his hands and his orange juice. "But she
left, she left me."

Henry's mother's smile fades slightly. "I think she's a
little like you. She was moving in her own story. But then there
was you and she was trapped in your tale."

Stories and tales and comic books, she's talking about
comic books, like your life is a comic book, and maybe it is.
No costumes, though. That's the new trend.

Stop it Carter. "Stop it."

"What's that, dear?"

"There has to be more than that. You came back, your
story was as important as Dad's, wasn't it? And you came
back." Your dad died. Her story included his death. Maybe
that's her story or an issue of her greater story. Your dad was
only a minor character. Maybe you're a minor character.
"Minor characters in the larger story. But whose story is it?"

She smiles again at her son, but not as radiant as before,
a twinge of age at the corners, something of the outside world
in her now.

Reading things into it again, just like she said. Stories and comics and psychobabble, nothing in the end. "Nothing at all," Henry whispers.

"I was just using the metaphor the woman used in her book. She used the story metaphor to get her point across."

"Metaphor?" You know about metaphors, no maybe you don't. They don't have those in Math and it's all about the math, isn't it? "No metaphors in Math."

"No, I suppose there isn't." She looks to the television and then back to Henry. "There is only what we make of the world. I thought you knew that."

Henry looks at her, the shadow of her nose, the slight darkness of her eyes, the wrinkles near her mouth. He sips his orange juice. The light from the television strobes the living room, giving the air a silver quality for a second, then dull gray, then back to silver.

"Oh my," his mother sighs and stands, her eyes fixed on the television. "My goodness."

"What?" Henry asks.

"Look at that." She finds the remote and Carter's voice becomes louder.

"Nearly one hundred bodies were found," Carter tells him. "The organization is known as the Knights of Christ, an extreme evangelical sect. Preliminary reports confirm an apparent mass suicide. Poison is believed the manner in which the members of this sect took their lives. All of them were found dressed in white gowns and seemingly died within moments of each other. The leader of the group left a recorded message." There is a pause. "Do we have it?" Carter asks an unseen sidekick. "We do? This was just released by the authorities."

Episode 33: Faith or Strength

A man's face appears on the screen. His skin is almost a pure white, his hair is an unnatural black, his dark eyes are without any real color and are set deeply in his face. His voice is high when he begins to speak, incongruous with his stern features.

"This is my testimony of the revealed word. God has given me this revelation in order to show his servants what must happen. Christ has made these things known to me through his angels. Happy are we who have heard this message and obey what has been foretold. For the time is near when all these things will happen."

He clears his throat as information continues to stream beneath him, random bits of the world: tensions, weather, sports, an alert about a missing child.

"We are of the 144,000 and we are called to his throne to praise him and reign with him in the world to come. This is the end for you. The seven seals have been broken by the Lamb, the four horses are free, the war has begun and all will be erased to be born again after the thousand years. The forty-two months end today and the worship of the two beasts is at an end. I have seen the three angels and heard their words:

'Fear God and give glory to His name, His judgment is at hand, she has fallen, great Babylon has fallen. Who ever bears the mark of the Beast will drink of God's wine, the wine of his fury.' This, I have been told. This I have seen."

"Oh dear," Henry's mother whispers. "Those poor people."

You see it don't you? "Yes." You're picking them out and doing the math in your head. "Yes, the numbers."

"What's that, Henry?"

"Nothing." The numbers.

The man sips from a bottle of water and the world continues beneath him in snippets of stories, scrolling along the bottom of the screen, endlessly moving forward. The man begins again. "Then the seven angels came and took me to the famous whore. I saw her sitting on a dragon and the dragon had seven heads and ten horns and the whore was dressed in purple and scarlet. The angels then said to me, 'This is Great America the mother of all perverts and whores of the world.' It was then that I understood my previous vision. Babylon has fallen. America has fallen."

Carter's voice cuts in. "We have a reporter on the scene. Let's go to Carter outside the temple."

"This is Carter outside the temple of the Knights of Christ." Carter stands before a stark white building, bathed in sunlight, apparently somewhere warm, the green grass, the swaying of the trees and the blue sky show a scene of comfort and of weather that is welcoming. Police cars dot the landscape, men in uniforms waltz behind Carter, short sleeved and unafraid of the coming cold. "We've just received some disturbing information about this morning's mass suicide. According to inside sources, there is strong evidence that several, perhaps a majority of the sect members were forced to drink the poisonous liquid or were outright murdered. The following video contains some graphic imagery."

The camera shakes as it moves down a corridor and stops at a door, an unknown hand pushes it open. There are five mats on the floor. A curtain is drawn over the sole window giving the scene a green gloom. The camera pans the room, the walls are bare except for a cross and a picture of the white-faced man. The camera moves across the floor where the bodies lie neatly in their white gowns, their arms folded over their chests. Eerily their eyes are open and their mouths are drawn into an expression between a gasp and an over emphasized smile

"You can see in this video various cells where members apparently slept and eventually died. Some cells contain up to ten bodies, some piled one on top of another. Authorities believe this might indicate resistance to the suicide pact. Reports are now coming in of members being bludgeoned to death as authorities piece together the last moments of the sect."

"Carter, this is Carter in the studio, is there any word on the leader of the cult?"

The screen flashes back to Carter standing outside the temple, the sun continues to shine as it would on any other day. The gathering crowd sports T-shirts and shorts and sunglasses, standing together in the warm air. Carter's skin is brown, his eyes glint, the sun is somewhere above him.

Henry stands rigid, the white-faced man still haunting his imagination. His mother whispers something about God. Henry turns from the television, refusing to watch the shaking green images or to listen to Carter's report on life and death in the sunshine and warm breeze. He walks away from the television, away from his mother, who remains staring at the images. In the kitchen, Henry finishes his orange juice and puts the glass in the sink. He gazes out the window, the world is growing dark and tomorrow is Christmas Eve.

His mother walks into the kitchen still muttering something about God. She is rummaging through her purse when she says, "What a tragedy. Those people they showed on that video… just terrible."

"Yes, yes it is," Henry whispers.

"I have to get going, dear. I'm meeting some old friends for dinner."

"Old friends?"

"Your father's and mine. We're going to talk about old times."

"Hmm."

"I'll be here tomorrow about four and we'll have Christmas Eve dinner."

Henry does not answer but continues to look out the window, at the snow, at the clouds, and thinking there must be warm sun behind them somewhere.

He can feel his mother's hand on his shoulder. "Are you sure you're all right, dear?"

He looks back at her, wrinkles about her mouth and eyes. They weren't there before she left, he thinks. Diana was the same, but his mother, she's different.

"I'm sorry, Mom. I haven't helped you with the arrangements for the funeral. I don't know what to do. I'll try harder."

She smiles at him, the radiant glowing smile of all mothers. "My dear boy, it's fine. You have to cope with your dad in your own way. I know this. Don't worry about any of the arrangements. Your dad and I planned everything years ago. It's all settled. You do what you need to do." She kisses him gently on the cheek and looks again into his face. Henry feels warm and comforted and safe and childish and loved.

His mother wraps her scarf about her shoulders and dons her heavy coat. "I'll see you tomorrow." She kisses him again and walks out into the cold and growing night. With her leaves Henry's sense of family and all the lovely things associated with his mother's smile.

Henry returns to the living room and shuts off the television. He notices the book on the coffee table. He picks it up and looks at the author's picture on the back. She seems younger in real life. The black and white photo accentuates the shadows of her eyes and nose, giving her an angular quality, like she's not real, like someone drew her in a highly stylized manner. He flips through the pages, stopping here and there, highlighted passages about happiness and pursuit, happiness in the abstract, happiness as concrete reality, the evolution of the right to be happy. He counts the number of times 'happy' appears in chapter six. The total is thirty-six which is six squared, and he smiles. He reads Diana's notes in the margins, her lovely handwriting, the swirl of her 's', the way her 'y' trails off, the simplistic beauty of her thought process. He loses himself in the combination of the hero principal's wife's philosophy and the additions made by beautiful Diana. He doesn't notice Arthur look in on him from time to time. He doesn't notice his son get his own dinner, a sandwich and some orange juice, doesn't notice Arthur eat his meal in the archway between the living room and the kitchen. Only when Arthur stands in front of him, does Henry look up from the book.

"It's bedtime, Dad," Arthur tells him.

"Is it?"

"Past, actually, it's eleven."

"Oh." Henry had turned on a light, but the rest of the house is dark, a deep and suffuse darkness. "Did you brush your teeth?"

"Yes."

"Oh goodness, your dinner." Henry stands suddenly and the book falls to the floor. Arthur touches his hand.

"It's okay, Dad. Grandma bought some groceries. I ate dinner."

"You did?"

"Yes."

Henry looks about the living room, not focusing on anything, not really looking for anything in particular. Arthur watches him and squeezes his hand tighter. "C'mon, Dad. It's time for bed."

Arthur leads his father. The boy hops into his bed and Henry stands over him.

"Would you like some music tonight?" Henry asks his son.

"No, not tonight."

Henry sits on the edge of the bed and helps his son arrange the pillows and blankets. "Are you excited for tomorrow?"

"Yes," Arthur responds as he makes the last few alterations: the blue blanket up to his knees, then the red and finally the yellow one.

"And how is your city?"

"I'm not sure. What will happen will happen with or without me. Just have to wait and see."

Henry kisses his son and turns off the light.

Episode 34: That My Eyes Could Look Through Thee

Henry enters the bathroom and turns on the light. The mirror looks at him, at his eyes that are young and old, at his mouth, at his nose, at his chin. He touches the image and runs his hand down the glass. He turns on the faucet and splashes water on his face. He shuts off the light and steps back into the bedroom. He throws his tie to the floor and unbuttons his shirt. He falls on the bed and bounces once, then comes to rest on her side. He rolls over onto his back and closes his eyes.

He sees a white building, stark against a perfect blue sky. There are people moving about, people in shorts and sunglasses. Carter is also there, holding a microphone.

Hello, Henry. I thought you might come back. I thought you saw it.

"I did."

So follow me as we enter the temple and investigate the last resting place of the Knights of Christ.

Henry frowns.

Too much? Have to sell it, though.

"I understand."

I call your attention to the outside of the building, it is the leader's, known as Pastor, his interpretation of the Temple of Solomon from Jerusalem. According to legend the temple is of note due to the fact that it is supposed to represent, in exact detail, heaven in terms of architecture and mathematical precision. Corners are at exact angles, each arch exactly the same, and the square footage can be reduced to the number thirty-three, which we know is the age of Christ when he was crucified.

"Fascinating."

I knew you would like that. Let's go in. Here in the receiving area we have a portrait of Pastor, looking stern, but if you pay close attention behind him, the background is shaded in light colors. This was done to show the path to heaven, a path that Pastor claimed to know. The frame measures 33 inches by 33 inches.

"Very interesting."

Beyond the receiving area we find the first chapel. It's the smallest of the three that are in the temple. This one is decorated with crosses and has the constant scent of incense funneled in. Here Pastor would meet potential converts. He would tell them of the upcoming rapture and of the end of the world. He also constantly referred to the other chapels, the more ornate places for prayer that are located further within the temple.

"Get their attention. Build their curiosity."

Just like teaching. Beyond the first chapel are several offices for the day-to-day business of the sect. Here secretaries bustled about with forms and the tasks of managing Pastor's assets. The majority of members tithed their personal savings to the sect. Even God needs to pay the overhead. This sacrifice was one of the final steps of becoming a member of the inner circle. Beyond the offices is where the real action took place.

"Action?"

Turn of phrase. But as we move deeper into the temple, the inner sanctums hold the greatest secrets. These initial sections beyond the façade of the offices were the living quarters of the newly converted. You see that the hall is rounded. Pastor was obsessed with circular patterns, the roundness of the shape, no points or angles, simply smooth. The entire interior is circular moving inward like a great swirl, a whirlpool if you will, drawn with quickening momentum to the center. And at the center was Pastor and his inner circle, those chosen from among the many to know him and the great destiny of the temple.

"That's a bit over the top."

Sorry, but sometimes I do get a touch dramatic.

"No problem. What's that?"

Oh that. Some of the newer converts needed to be shown the path to salvation.

"Shown?"

A club or a bat most likely. You can imagine the frenzy of those last moments. Only hours left in the life of the world, a world that had turned wicked and cold. The signs aligning to show the horrible truth. Some of the newer ones, the yet to be indoctrinated questioned Pastor's reading of the omens. They dared to say that it might be something other than the absolute truth. Denial of the end. It was probably very sad. Those who believed had to take action. Souls were in peril after all. It had to be done. The faithless were forced to face the light, such as it was.

"The blood?"

Yes, so much of it. On the walls. On the ceiling. The pools of it on the floor. But it's the end of the world and subtlety is no longer required.

"Horrible, horrible, horrible."

Truly and more than that. They were left here to bleed to death, brains dripping on the ground, struggling perhaps. The height of the evolution of man falls formless on the cold floor. The struggle ends without glamour, without fanfare. These poor creatures in search of connection only to find their end in a cold room with strangers.

"Are you trying to make a point?"

No point to this. Nothing but the end of lives and better men than me have tried to make something more out of this. We move on. The corridors start to double in on themselves as we move deeper. The discarded instruments of faith can be seen, left for others to ponder over. A stray body of one who might have fled only to be caught and purified. And we move on. As you glance through the small windows of the passing cell doors you'll see any manner of how people met the great beyond. Several had formed intimate bonds and reached for one another at the end. You can see them touching, a final embrace, clichéd and beautiful.

"Their faces..."

Ghastly, but a moment of pain and then peace.

"Assuming it is peaceful."

True and we move on. You see some chose to die alone, holding their death pose. Few are in the halls, perhaps tricked into drinking the elixir or maybe making a last ditch effort to die in the sun. Various poses, various people, a myriad of men and women, a world onto itself.

"Death isn't poetic."

Death is the only real poem.

"That's stupid."

So it is and we move on. We're getting closer to the center, moving inward along the spiral. You can see there seems to be a lack of corpses immediately before the inner chambers. We pause before the great door and contemplate what lies beyond.

"We have to continue."

Do we?

"Yes."

Why?

"You know why."

Maybe she's not here.

"I have to be sure. For Arthur."

She wouldn't be part of the inner circle. She left them. She would not be welcomed back.

"Where is she then?"

Who knows? Maybe she tried to stop it. Maybe she got a call from a friend who knew it was getting bad and this friend wanted out like Diana. Maybe Diana went to this friend. Maybe she was drawn back in. Maybe all the inner circle was allowed to say goodbye before the end and this was her way of telling you goodbye. Maybe she really believed.

"Maybe, maybe, maybe."

That's all we have.

"What about Pastor? What about Sekowsky?"

What about him?

"Maybe he escaped. Maybe it was a giant con that got out of hand. Maybe they killed him when they learned the truth. Maybe they crucified him. Maybe Diana led the charge. Maybe she was a hero. But maybe Pastor believed. Maybe he was right."

You don't believe that.

"Don't I?"

The bedroom has grown black. The wind blows against the windows and snow flutters up to the sky. The cold settles on the house and the furnace constantly runs to keep it at bay. The windows have spider-web ice lines and are fogged near the baseboards where the processed heat emerges from the basement. The streetlights highlight the falling snow, descending in earnest. The neighborhood sleeps and bundles itself in the hope that this is just another false alarm and tomorrow won't be much different than today. Henry lies on his back, refusing to dive beneath the covers, refusing to shiver, refusing to be moved until he wants to move. He thinks that this is his statement to the world, it will know that he did not wrap himself in warmth until he was ready. The world will remember this act of defiance when all else is gone.

"It does have a point. You were wrong about that."

Was I?

"Yes. It's the biggest point of them all. It's everything. When anyone dies it's the end of the world."

That was poetic. You never liked English.

"I was wrong about death. It is poetic, like math is poetic, like all things are poetic, meaning and hidden meaning. The grand point of the world."

That sounds like nonsense.

"It is and that's the point. The nonsense we believe is important."

Henry opens his eyes and the bedroom is there and Diana is not. He removes his clothes and pulls the blankets over his head. His breath is warm and the sheets are cold. He shivers, wrapping his arms around his knees.

"This is us at the end of the world."

Episode 35: Doomsday

Arthur wakes later than normal. His eyes adjust and he yawns. He gets out of bed and walks to the bathroom. He brushes his teeth and gurgles water and spits. He walks to the kitchen, the light is on. He smells coffee and the orange juice container is on the counter. He stretches and cracks his neck. Must've slept wrong. He pours a glass of juice and sits at the table. After three sips he has an urge to look outside.

He strolls with purpose to the front door. He opens it after some effort. The snow on the front porch melds into the snow on the front yard to form one giant picture of white. The air is very cold and his breath fogs. Decorations can still be seen here and there under the snow. Christmas Eve today, almost forgot. The street seems clean, erased in places. Small twirls of smoke from chimneys curl into the blue sky. Children can be heard in the distance.

Arthur steps into the snow and sinks nearly to his waist. Not cold, not really cold at all. With some effort, Arthur jumps, almost clearing the snow and falls into a white mound, making a shallow grave. He lays there until the cold seeps into his skin and then he rises and returns to the house. He changes his clothes, shivering slightly and he goes to find his father.

Henry is sitting in the basement. His coffee steams, a thin white mist. The city lies in ruins before him. The buildings have fallen in on themselves and people lie scattered in the street. Some of the larger buildings that once towered over Central City, made of sipping-straw infrastructures are hanging open, the skeleton of plastic exposed, papier-mâché hanging off like so much skin. The spires of the city, monuments to ingenuity and imagination are split and seem ready to fall. The orange light of the heater casts a haze over the city, the dawn of the day after. The buildings seem as black ghosts in the light. Gotham is awash with fallen towers and the quaint neighborhoods are a maze of destruction. The people, all the lovely and different people are piled against one another in a ghastly display of community and death. There seems no reason or path to the destruction. Henry looks up at Arthur as he comes down the stairs.

Before the boy gets to the last stair, Henry asks, "What happened?"

Arthur looks about the basement. "It ended."

"What?"

"It came to an end. They felt it and I felt it. It was time to move on. I wasn't that interested in it anymore. I don't need it anymore."

"Don't need it?"

"No, not anymore."

"What happened to all the people?"

"I threw most of them out."

"Threw them out?"

"Yes. I'm not sure what I'll do with the rest of it. I like some of the buildings. I think I might like to be an architect or something like that. I liked planning out the city. It was fun."

"Fun?"

"Yes. Thinking of what to put in next. Where a building should go, making room. It was fun for a while."

"You did plan it, didn't you?"

"Yes."

"Thought it through, measured it, planned it, did the math."

"Yes."

"But in the end you just smashed it."

"It was getting too big. Besides I should be thinking about school. Mom told me that I should work harder at school. She said it's important."

"Did she?"

"Yes."

"And where is she now?"

"I don't know."

Arthur walks around the tables. He passes the beach, where people in a heap near the imaginary seashore. On the edge of Gotham a large building has fallen over but remains intact, creating a barrier between one section and the next. Henry sips his coffee. Arthur stands next to him.

"And what should we do with all of this?" Henry asks.

"I'll clean it up," Arthur answers. He looks up at his father. "Are you all right, Dad?"

Henry looks down at his son and smiles. He kisses the top of the boy's head. "I'm fine."

Arthur doesn't smile in return. "I'm going to get some breakfast. Would you like some breakfast?"

"No, thank you."

Arthur walks back upstairs, leaving his father alone with only the hum of the heater as company.

"It ended," Henry whispers.

So it has.

"But is this the end, the final ending? Is this the world ending?"

Everyday is an ending. Each moment brings us closer to the end.

"Depressing."

That it is. Remember when you would run away and fight dragons?

"Yes. What does that have to do with this?"

Nothing.

"I see."

Arthur pauses at the top of the stairs and listens to his father mumble.

Arthur wanders about the house, seeing it for the first time. He looks out the window at the snow and the ice. He eats his cereal and drinks his orange juice. He watches television, cartoons, a cat and a mouse, severe bodily damage and the cat survives to fight again. He answers the phone and talks to his grandmother, she'll stop by later for Christmas Eve dinner. The phone rings again.

"Hello," Arthur answers.

"Hello this is Agent Strange from the FBI."

"The FBI?"

"Yes." There's a pause. "Who am I speaking with?"

"Arthur Kent."

"How old are you Arthur?"

"Why?"

Agent Strange clears his throat. "Is your dad there?"

"He's not feeling well right now."

"Could you get him?"

"I'm afraid I can't. He's very sick. My grandma is coming over to take care of him."

"Oh." There are whispers on Agent Strange's end. "Could you take down my number and have your grandmother call me." There is another pause and more whispers. "He's just a kid. I can't ask him. I know. I know it's important. Fine." Agent Strange clears his throat. "Arthur, do you think you could answer some questions?"

"Sure. Do you still want my grandma to call you when she gets here?"

"Yes. You have to listen carefully now. Can you do that?"

"Yes."

"Good, that's good. Have you talked to your mom lately?"

"No."

"When was the last time you saw her?"

"Three days ago."

"Where is she?"

"I don't know. She got a phone call and left."

"Do you know who called her?"

"No."

"Have you ever heard your mother mention someone named Sekowsky?"

"No."

"Are you sure?"

"Yes."

There are more whispers on Agent Strange's end. "Arthur?"

"Yes."

"Did you ever hear your mom mention something called The Knights of Christ or see anything with those words on it? You can read, can't you?"

"Yes, I can read," Arthur responds, insulted. "But I've never heard my mom say those words or read those words on anything she had."

"Arthur." Henry appears in the living room. "Who are you talking to?"

"The FBI."

"The FBI?"

"Yes."

"Who are you talking to, Arthur?" Agent Strange asks.

"My dad."

"Can I talk to him?"

"Dad, the FBI wants to talk to you." Arthur hands Henry the phone.

"Hello," Henry says quietly.

"Mr. Kent?"

"Yes."

"You son said you were sick."

"He did?" Henry looks at his son. Arthur shrugs his shoulders and walks away. "What's this about?"

"It's about your wife. Have you heard from her recently?"

Henry pauses and looks at the television. A mouse is hitting a cat with a frying pan. "With whom am I speaking?"

"This is Agent Strange. Would you like more verification?"

"No." Henry listens to the wind push against the house. "My wife was home about three days ago, then she left."

"Do you know where she is?"

"No."

"Are you sure?"

"Yes." The cat is chasing the mouse with a shotgun.

"I'm going to level with you, Mr. Kent. You've no doubt heard about the Knights of Christ mass suicide?"

"I have."

"We have reason to believe that your wife was once a member of that cult."

"Hmm." The cat fires the shotgun but misses, blowing a hole in a door.

"Mr. Kent?"

"Is she dead?"

Agent Strange pauses. "We're not sure at the present time. Her body was not among those found at the temple. This is sensitive information. There seems to be some inconsistencies with several of the members of the inner circle, including Sekowsky."

"Hmm."

"One of the members of this inner circle was found late last night. There are indications Sekowsky may be alive."

"What does this have to do with my wife?"

"We're not sure. That's why we'd like to find her and ask her some questions."

"As I've said, I haven't seen her in days."

"Is that normal for her?"

"What are you implying?"

"Nothing, Mr. Kent. It does seem odd, however, that your wife comes home and then leaves again and you have no idea where she is."

"Is that odd?" Henry asks.

"Mr. Kent?"

"Yes."

"I'll ask this again, do you know where your wife is?"

"No."

Agent Strange sighs. "Would you take down my number and call me if you hear from her?"

"Yes." Henry listens to the numbers and responds with soft grunts, but does not write anything down.

"Thank you, Mr. Kent." The line goes dead.

In his mind he adds the digits of the phone number and then he subtracts them, divides them, multiplies them, a square root, a factor of three, but there is nothing in them he decides. Just numbers, just a phone number, like everyone else's number, nothing secret, nothing mysterious, just a number provided by the phone company, nothing important. He shoulders slump slightly.

Arthur has reappeared and stands before him, his head cocked to one side. "It's Christmas Eve, Dad."

"Yes," Henry responds.

"Grandma is coming over for dinner?"

"She'll make dinner. She always makes dinner on Christmas Eve. We should go shopping."

"We went yesterday."

"What?"

"We went yesterday."

"Then she'll cook dinner, like she used to do when I was a boy. When my dad was alive."

"Hmm."

Henry pats Arthur on the head and returns to the basement. Arthur watches him, stepping slowly, carefully down the stairs. Arthur waits until his father is out of sight and then he returns to the living room.

The television is still on and Arthur sits on the floor in front of it. He switches to the twenty-four hour news station. He finds something familiar about anchor's face. He watches scenes from around the world. He sees people in Europe as they talk about fighting for the right reasons. Arthur knows their thoughts suddenly, as if a light has been turned on in a dark room. Their thoughts are turning back to past wars and the agony and the pain, but the eventual victory and then everything will be all right afterward. The next scene is from China and these people seem unconcerned about the upcoming war. If it happens then it will and then the consequences will be handled. The next scene is from the Middle East and the absolute knowledge of right and everyone else must be wrong.

Countless faces pass before him and he knows them in some way or another, their pasts, their futures, what they'll say next and he knows he could always do this; read and understand people and suddenly he makes sense to himself. He watches the words scroll along the bottom of the screen, snippets of life passing along and then off to the right. There is a blizzard in Kansas, flooding in Oregon, a wild fire in Florida. There's a new economic policy in place for low-income families. Arthur's eyes glance up at the pictures and then back to the words. People are screaming and running through the streets and a football player has beaten his wife. Bombs are being dropped with great accuracy and a new holiday movie opens in theaters today. He switches the channel to a local station. The pretty anchorwoman mentions the end of the world and then the weatherman begins to explain that it will snow tomorrow. Then the pretty woman is back and talks of a missing child, runaway or something more sinister. And it all makes sense finally, it all falls into place and Arthur watches it

213

all unfold before him.

<<<>>>

Arthur's grandmother comes through the door at five in the evening.

"Merry Christmas, Arthur," she calls to him.

Arthur trots to the kitchen and embraces her tightly. "Merry Christmas, Grandma."

"How are you, my dear?"

"I'm fine. How are you?"

She smiles and kisses the top his head. "I'm fine too. I have some presents for you." She produces several bags of wrapped boxes of various shapes. "Would you put these under the tree for me?"

"Sure." Arthur follows his grandmother's request and returns to the kitchen.

"Where's your father?"

"In the basement."

She turns and opens the basement door. Arthur pauses and stands close behind her. They descend together.

Henry is sitting on the edge of the tables, far in the corner. Behind him is a tool bench where Henry used to make things, cabinets and such, before Arthur needed the space. The heater hums and the small overhead lamp provides a dim light. Arthur and his grandmother stop at the bottom of the stairs.

"Merry Christmas, Henry," his mother calls out through the cold basement.

Henry doesn't look up. He remains seated staring at the tables. The buildings that had fallen and the people that were piled here and there are gone. The tables are a clean slate, nothing remains of the once grand society that had laid claim to the picnic table and the card table and the sawhorses. The buildings that were designed by a genius hand, the hidden symbols of Gotham, the high towers of Central City, the marvelous atmosphere of Coast City have been erased by another immortal hand. Intricacies and secrets, lives and histories gone forever, like some cardboard Atlantis. The people of the before, the lives of the Gods who were here and then vanished are like the myths of Greece and Rome and those lesser known worlds that existed and perished before it was important to know about the past. Life in all its wonder existed and now doesn't. That's what was and is no longer. Lives will be built in this new world and the city that was will be as a whisper, a story, as if it never was real.

Henry moves slowly, placing something in front of him and then sits back. Arthur takes his grandmother's hand and leads her to his father. They stand next to him and look down at the table.

"Is that our house?" Arthur asks.

"Yes," Henry answers.

"And that's me and Grandma and you?"

"Yes."

Arthur scans the table. There is a high school and people stand about it. There is a man in a lab coat, an older man next to a pretty woman, a police officer, two other men in ties. A group of pre-teenage boys are set up near a building that once was an abandoned warehouse in Gotham. They seem to have bits of tape holding them together, as if they had been torn apart and fixed and torn again. Arthur remembers that they disappeared from his city some time ago. One might have been Mrs. Grayson's son and another looks like the picture of the boy that the pretty anchorwoman said was missing. A larger group of adults stand in a circle with a man dressed as a priest in the center. The hero principal stands apart, as if he might be watching everything come into existence.

"Is that Mom, in your hand?" Arthur asks.

Henry looks down at the cut out picture. He moves it slightly, holding it as if it were some rare gem. "Yes." Henry leans over the table and places the picture next to pictures of himself and Arthur. He sits back. "She's going to be a hero, I think. She'll catch a very bad man, her nemesis. Do you know

215

what that word means, Arthur? I'll tell you about it some day. I'll explain everything to you some day."

People stand before Henry in the burgeoning suburb, which will grow as houses are built, parks are placed here and there, schools for all the children, malls and bars, theaters and graveyards for those who lived here before, because special places have histories. And everyone will have a past. There will be heroes with gray backgrounds, conflicted women who struggle against society, broken warriors with no wars to fight, tragic children trapped by their own bodies, mysterious little girls who look at the world through reflective glasses, wives with hidden passions, and more and more people, infinite in desires and needs. And all this will grow before him.

Footsteps can be heard on the stairs, shoes moving down, click and click. Then emerging from the dull light is radiant Diana, beautiful Diana. She's smiling. Henry is smiling. Henry's mother is smiling at her son, touching the back of his head, gently and motherly.

Henry whispers to his suburb, "This is not us at the end of the world. This is us at the beginning of the world."

Arthur forces his lips to curve, forces the emotion to the surface and he, very slowly, smiles.

- End

The Author

Mark Pogodzinski lives in Buffalo, New York with his lovely wife and their dogs. His other works include *The Valley of Ashes* and *The Ceremony of Innocence*.